Skills

Superspeed, Ancient ~~
Combo Blade, Defens~~
Gale Slash, Down Attack, Power Attack, ~~
Fire Ball, Water Ball
Wind Cutter, Cyclone Cutter
Sand Cutter, Dark Ball
Water Wall, Wind Wall, Refresh, Heal

SALLY'S STATS

Sally

Lv24   HP 32/32   MP 80/80

[STR 55]   [VIT 0]
[AGI 153] [DEX 45]
[INT 50]

Bofuri

★I Don't★ Want to Get Hurt, so I'll ② Max Out My Defense.

YUUMIKAN

Illustration by KOIN

YEN ON
NEW YORK

Welcome to
NewWorld Online.

Bofuri I Don't Want to Get Hurt, so I'll Max Out My Defense.

YUUMIKAN

Translation by Andrew Cunningham • Cover art by KOIN

This book is a work of fiction. Names, characters, places, and incidents are the product of the author's imagination or are used fictitiously. Any resemblance to actual events, locales, or persons, living or dead, is coincidental.

ITAINO WA IYA NANODE BOGYORYOKU NI KYOKUFURI SHITAITO OMOIMASU. Vol. 2
©Yuumikan, KOIN 2017
First published in Japan in 2017 by KADOKAWA CORPORATION, Tokyo.
English translation rights arranged with KADOKAWA CORPORATION, Tokyo, through TUTTLE-MORI AGENCY, INC., Tokyo.

English translation © 2021 by Yen Press, LLC

Yen Press, LLC supports the right to free expression and the value of copyright. The purpose of copyright is to encourage writers and artists to produce the creative works that enrich our culture.

The scanning, uploading, and distribution of this book without permission is a theft of the author's intellectual property. If you would like permission to use material from the book (other than for review purposes), please contact the publisher. Thank you for your support of the author's rights.

Yen On
150 West 30th Street, 19th Floor
New York, NY 10001

Visit us at yenpress.com • facebook.com/yenpress • twitter.com/yenpress
yenpress.tumblr.com • instagram.com/yenpress

First Yen On Edition: June 2021

Yen On is an imprint of Yen Press, LLC.
The Yen On name and logo are trademarks of Yen Press, LLC.

The publisher is not responsible for websites (or their content) that are not owned by the publisher.

Library of Congress Cataloging-in-Publication Data
Names: Yuumikan, author. I Koin, illustrator. I Cunningham, Andrew, 1979– translator.
Title: Bofuri, I don't want to get hurt, so I'll max out my defense / Yuumikan ; illustration by Koin ; translated by Andrew Cunningham.
Other titles: Itai no wa Iya nano de bōgyoryoku ni kyokufuri shitai to omoimasu. English
Description: First Yen On edition. I New York : Yen On, 2021–
Identifiers: LCCN 2020055872 I ISBN 9781975322731 (v. 1 ; trade paperback) I
    ISBN 9781975323547 (v. 2 ; trade paperback)
Subjects: LCSH: Video gamers—Fiction. I Virtual reality—Fiction. I GSAFD: Science fiction.
Classification: LCC PL874.I46 I8313 2021 I DDC 895.63/6—dc23
LC record available at https://lccn.loc.gov/2020055872

ISBNs: 978-1-9753-2354-7 (paperback)
       978-1-9753-2355-4 (ebook)

10 9 8 7 6 5 4 3 2 1

LSC-C

Printed in the United States of America

CONTENTS

**I Don't Want to Get Hurt,
so I'll Max Out My Defense.**

⊹ Chapter 1	Defense Build and the Second Event	001	⊹
⊹ Chapter 2	Defense Build and Resuming Exploration	019	⊹
⊹ Chapter 3	Defense Build and the Transport Destination	043	⊹
⊹ Intermission	Defense Build and Admins	059	⊹
⊹ Chapter 4	Defense Build and Late-Night Exploration	063	⊹
⊹ Chapter 5	Defense Build and Canyon Exploration	077	⊹
⊹ Chapter 6	Defense Build and Downstream Exploration	093	⊹
⊹ Intermission	Defense Build and Admins 2	113	⊹
⊹ Chapter 7	Defense Build and Desert Exploration	115	⊹
⊹ Intermission	Defense Build and Admins 3	131	⊹
⊹ Chapter 8	Defense Build and Encounters	133	⊹
⊹ Chapter 9	Defense Build and the Event's Fifth Day	153	⊹
⊹ Chapter 10	Defense Build and the Squid Hunt	183	⊹
⊹ Chapter 11	Defense Build and the Event's Sixth Day	199	⊹
⊹ Chapter 12	Defense Build and Skill Selection	219	⊹
⊹ Intermission	Defense Build and Admins 4	235	⊹
⊹ Epilogue	Defense Build and the Spoils of Battle	239	⊹
⊹ Afterword		247	

CHAPTER 1

Defense Build and the Second Event

"Time for the event!"

"Heh-heh. You nervous, Maple?"

"Nope! I'm all good."

As the two girls talked, they drew plenty of looks from the crowd. Players decked out in all kinds of gear were gathering in the square, waiting for the start signal.

Maple's real name was Kaede Honjou. Her best friend, Risa Shiromine, had suggested they play *NewWorld Online* together, but Kaede didn't know much about games. As a result, she'd created an extreme build heavily focused on defense, and a series of happy accidents had earned her some powerful skills. She was now so tanky, it had made her rather famous.

And today was the game's second big event. This time, Risa—aka Sally—was joining in.

Sally and Maple were in the second stratum's town.

They'd done everything they could to get ready for the event and were raring for action.

All that was left was to wait breathlessly, urging the clock forward.

Then Maple spotted a familiar face in the crowd.

"Oh! Be right back, Sally!" she said before stepping away. "Chrome! How's it been?"

"Mm? Oh, Maple! Long time no see."

When Maple had been trying to make a better great shield, Chrome had introduced her to a crafter named Iz. Like Maple, he was a great shielder, and a powerful one—he'd come in ninth in the previous event.

"This event's gonna be so much fun!"

"You bet. I'm sure you'll do real well, Maple."

A few more words, and Maple headed over to Sally's side.

"Hey, Sally, I'm back. Is it time yet?"

"Should be. Place's getting packed."

The crowd had grown exponentially larger, and the noise level was rising accordingly.

And just as it seemed there was no more room left, the admin's voice rang out.

"Today's event is all about exploration! Your objective is to collect the three hundred silver medals scattered across the map. Every set of ten earns you a gold medal! At the end of the event, you can exchange gold medals for skills or equipment."

Everyone's status menus opened automatically, displaying examples of silver and gold medals.

Maple had seen the gold medals before.

She'd earned one in the first event but had assumed it was just a keepsake medal.

"The top ten players of the first event already have one gold medal! Defeat them, and their medals are yours! Or simply explore to your heart's content!"

Now the status screens showed a number of fancy rings and bracelets, as well as swords, bows, and other weapons. These, too, were apparently scattered across the event map.

There were definitely some great shields in the mix.

All players were also sent a message detailing the medal compensation rule. Players who'd earned a gold medal in the first event had targets painted on their backs, but if their medals were stolen and they failed to recover them before the event ended, they'd be rewarded five silver medals to make up for it.

"If you die, medals are the only thing you'll lose! Don't worry—your gear will be totally safe! And even then, medals will only drop if you're defeated by another player. So get on out there and explore! Should you die, you'll respawn at your starting location."

That was certainly a relief.

If there was no chance of losing gear, that made it easier to take greater risks.

Anyone could explore anywhere and any way they wanted.

"This event will last a week in-game. But time will be sped up, so it'll only take two external hours! There are several areas on the map where no monsters appear, so make good use of them."

They'd get to spend a week exploring and sleeping inside the game, but only a fraction of that time would pass in the real world.

"It's a bit weird when you stop to think about it."

"Log out at all and you can't rejoin the event. If you wanna see it through, you've gotta stay logged in! And...yup, if you're all in the same party, you'll get sent to the same place."

As they listened to the explanation, Sally and Maple went

over the details on their status screens. Naturally, neither of them planned to log out until the event was complete.

"Hopefully, we can find enough medals for both of us!"

"Yup! Let's go for it!"

Their bodies turned to light, vanishing from the second stratum square.

"Hmm…guess this is it?"

"Looks like."

They could feel the ground beneath their feet.

The pair found themselves standing in the center of a grassy field.

Floating islands dotted the air up above, seemingly unfettered by gravity's influence. In the distance, mountain peaks loomed. Dragons elegantly soared through the clear skies.

The map prepared for this event was one filled with natural splendor—perfect for monsters.

An idyllic landscape, the kind of fantasy world everyone dreams about.

"Wow! It's beautiful!"

"Whoa…! This is breathtaking."

The two girls set out across the field. They walked a good twenty minutes without even catching sight of any other players. Last time, Maple hadn't needed to wait very long before her first encounter, so this map was clearly *much* bigger.

"I wonder how we're going to find some medals…"

"Good question. It's not like we're in a rush, though. We've got plenty of time."

Their discussion was interrupted by a pack of goblins prowling the low grass on their right. The girls veered left, but the goblins followed—clearly targeting them.

"If it's just goblins, I'd better use White Snow."

Maple swapped out her great shield. She only had so many uses of Devour a day, and it didn't make sense to waste them.

She had the Devour skill equipped on her usual shield, Night's Facsimile. Anything that touched it would take damage and be converted into MP. This had made Maple so absurdly powerful that the last patch had added a use limit to the skill—specifically to nerf Maple.

"I guess I should stick to this for now? I can always swap to Night's Facsimile if I need it."

"Sounds good! You do you. For now, I'll make quick work of these guys."

Sally darted toward the goblins with her daggers at the ready. Moving like the wind, she dodged their attacks while landing her own swift and accurate blows. Sally had gone for the opposite of Maple's build and left her Vitality at zero, sacrificing all defense for an Agility-focused build. Her style was completely based on dodge and counter—if enemies never hit her, she never took damage. A goblin tried to block her strikes with its club, but such meager weaponry was no match for her daggers.

The club fell from the goblin's hands as a red line ran across its body.

A moment later, it vanished in a shower of light.

"Oh! You're so fast!"

"Heh-heh-heh, thanks. Seems like this area only has weak monsters. Doubt we'll find a medal here."

"Hmm, you may be right. I bet they're hidden in less obvious places."

Sally nodded in reply, and they started checking for nearby caves or forests—anywhere that seemed like it could be home to a ton of monsters.

They'd walked on for about an hour.

"Grass on the right! Grass on the left! Grass behind us! Grass before us!"

Sally was getting frustrated. The prairie seemed to go on forever. That was the only thing they could see all the way up to the horizon.

"It's too big... We haven't even fought anything but goblins... Ugh, there's another one."

Maple pointed. A goblin was dragging a rabbit across the field—it must have been out hunting. Judging by how it was cackling happily to itself, the monster hadn't noticed the girls yet. Goblin voices really grated on the ears.

But as they watched, it walked straight forward—and sank into the ground.

""......Huh?""

This left them momentarily stunned, but they soon recovered and moved to investigate.

"There's nothing here?"

"No, there's gotta be! Somewhere!"

Sally had an idea, and she cast Wind Cutter.

This sliced through the visual distortion, restoring the original landscape.

Her attack revealed a set of stairs descending into the earth at their feet.

"Looks like they used something like my Mirage skill to disguise the entrance to their lair... Seems like this may not be the only one, either... It *is* a pretty big prairie."

"Should we go in?"

"Of course! Anything this well hidden's gotta have a medal or two inside!"

"Cool! Let's go!"

They plunged into the cavern below.

"Ho…kay!"

They found a goblin immediately inside, and Sally stabbed it right in the face.

The monsters here weren't particularly strong, so Sally made swift work of everything else they encountered.

The paths were wide enough for the two of them to walk side by side, and they could swing their weapons unhindered.

"Another fork," Maple muttered.

She was grumbling for a reason. This cave had a *lot* of branching paths. They ran all over the place, like an ant farm, and most of them led to dead ends.

"Hmm, which way…? You wanna pick this time, Maple?"

"…Right, I guess? It slopes down. If there's a boss here, we'll probably find it somewhere deeper."

"Works for me. Right it is."

They headed farther down the path and soon found themselves in a larger room.

And then…

A howl echoed through the cave. The floor shook.

Both girls realized instantly that the noise came from a boss.

Footsteps. Metal clanking. Fearsome growls. And the sounds were coming closer.

*　　*　　*

"The boss might've called for reinforcements, because I can already see some goblins coming!"

"What do we do?"

Sally raised her daggers.

"Only two ways into this room! That one's yours!"

"Okay! I got it covered!"

Maple didn't switch shields.

She figured she should save Devour for the boss.

Instead, she drew New Moon.

And so the battle began.

"Hydra!"

Purple light poured out of Maple's short sword, followed by a torrent of poison (shaped like a three-headed dragon) that raced toward the approaching pack of goblins. This poison was so powerful, the only way to avoid damage was with a Poison Nullification–level skill.

Maple was going all out from the get-go. Her maximum MP was very low, and a lot of her skills and magic had use limits to boot. This meant the more times she attacked, the less options she'd have to deal damage later. So whenever she could, she tried to kill monsters in a single blow.

But as Maple's Hydra rushed toward the goblin wave, it was blocked by a glittering wall.

Behind the goblin horde were three goblins wielding staffs and hats pulled low over their eyes.

The magic wall must've been their doing. If they could cast that spell every time, Sally was worried it might pose a serious problem—but fortunately, that was a needless concern.

Summoning that wall clearly took a lot out of them—all three goblin mages were breathing heavily.

Or maybe Maple's attack was simply that strong.

And the Hydra did more than just rush at foes.

The wall may have blocked the impact, but the resulting poison remained.

When the goblins stepped in it, they howled in pain and vanished in a puff of light.

But before their compatriots died, other goblins used their bodies as stepping stones, crossing the sea of poison safely.

It would take more than a few deaths to slow their advance—perhaps they were unable to disobey an order from the boss.

"Shield Attack!"

Maple's skill did very little damage, but it had a strong knockback effect, which she took full advantage of to push the goblins into the poison.

Repeating this action was all Maple had to do to chip away at the goblin horde. She'd been worried the three mages might start casting support spells, but it seemed they were already out of gas.

"Shield Attack! And that's the last one!"

As Maple's battle wound down, Sally came to check on her, having already wrapped up her own fight.

She spotted the three mages at the back of the passage and quickly started casting. "Fire Ball! And Wind Cutter!"

The goblin mages seemed to have little in the way of defense, and the spells easily finished them off.

"Nice work, Sally!"

"You too, Maple. Those were some impressive moves."

Sally raised an eyebrow at the lake of poison.

"Ha-ha-ha, yeah..." Maple grinned bashfully, then quickly

changed the subject. "Let's keep going. The boss room must be this way!"

"Yeah, good idea. Hup!"

Sally jumped forward, easily clearing the poison pond. Maple simply walked through it. Her Poison Resist was flawless.

"I'd be dead if a single drop of that touched me!"

It was impossible for a party member's spell to damage you directly, but residual effects were a different story.

If a Fire Ball lit up a tree and a teammate grabbed the burning branches, they'd definitely be hurt.

"Careful."

"Always."

They headed down the passage…where the real fight awaited.

"That sure looks like a boss room!"

There was a door in front of them—the only one in the underground passage. It was a good five yards tall, made of wood, and decorated in a way that gave it the distinct vibe that a boss fight lay on the other side.

Maple and Sally pushed it open and stepped inside.

The space beyond was dimly lit.

The ceiling was twice as tall as the door, and the width of the room was much the same.

But the farther in they went, the more it opened up. At the very back was a massive throne.

And seated atop was a very ugly goblin.

It was hard to judge the creature's height when it was sitting down, but it was at least as tall as the door—three times the size of your average goblin.

When it saw the girls enter, it bellowed.

The noise was so loud, both of them winced.

"Let's beat this thing quickly! Before it blows out our ears!"

"Completely agree!" Sally nodded.

Maple switched her shield to Night's Facsimile, and they were ready to go.

There were a good twenty yards between them and the goblin.

Sally tried to close that distance at speed.

But the goblin didn't let her.

It picked up a giant saber lying beside the throne and stepped forward, swinging it savagely.

A gust of wind shot toward Sally, followed by the blade itself.

"Cover Move! Cover!"

Maple wasn't sure if Sally could successfully dodge or not. The saber's blade was twice as long as she was tall, but Maple stood before it undaunted, her great shield raised. The blade struck—and vanished. Devour had converted it to MP. The awesome destructive force of their foe's main weapon was instantly eliminated in a shower of light.

"Nice! My turn..."

Sally never stopped running. But what Maple did next surprised both her and the boss.

"Cover Move!"

Despite Sally's speed, Maple instantly caught up with her. The goblin didn't even get a chance to attack.

Sally kept going. She had not expected Maple to move like that, but she couldn't stop now.

"Cover Move!"

Once again, Maple activated her skill, using brute force to reach Sally's position. This brought both of them right in front of the goblin.

The boss's muscles rippled, and with a crash, it swung its fists down at them.

But the attack missed Sally entirely.

With her evasive skills, no attack that telegraphed would ever hit home. She turned her dodge into a leap, taking aim at the monster's belly.

Just as Sally's daggers were about to hit...

"Cover Move!"

This was so removed from what that skill had been designed to do that Sally couldn't help but laugh.

But now Maple was inches from the goblin boss—meaning her great shield could reach it.

Sally landed her blow and leaped back.

Maple put her back into it, swinging her shield.

"Well? Strong enough for you?"

The entire length of her shield slammed into the goblin's belly. Damage effects sprayed everywhere, and a full 30 percent of its HP drained away.

This seemed to infuriate the goblin, and it punched Maple, knocking her to the ground.

"Mwa-ha-ha! Double damage? Double zero is still zero!"

The usual downside to Cover Move was that the user would take twice as much damage after activating the skill. Maple's raw defense stats were so off the charts that they simply negated that. But this was not the case for her armor—there was a *snap*, and a web of cracks ran across the surface.

"Eep?!"

Maple let out a squeak, and her shattered armor glowed... before instantly returning to normal.

"Oh! Right! Destructive Growth!"

When her equipment broke, it got stronger and more durable.

"You good for another run?" Sally called.

"One hundred percent!"

Maple scrambled to her feet, watching Sally start her approach.

Just as the goblin's fist seemed about to hit her...

"Cover Move! Cover!"

Maple appeared between the fist and Sally, great shield held high.

The shield instantly swallowed up a chunk of the goblin's arm. Red sparks sprayed everywhere. The boss had swung as hard as it could, trying to land a hit on a fast-moving target—and couldn't stop the punch in time.

Once again, its HP gauge took a huge hit.

It was at 40 percent health now.

Maple drew New Moon.

"I've gotta get a few blows in, too!" Sally yelled. "Superspeed!"

Her body blurred. She was now running even faster.

She raced around the goblin to strike from the rear.

"Double Slash! Wind Cutter! Power Attack! Double Slash!"

Superspeed's effect made her attacks faster, too. But this flurry of blows carved off only 10 percent of the boss's health bar—which just proved how ridiculous Maple's shield really was.

Still, this was enough to make the goblin shift its attention toward Sally.

As it turned, it raised an arm. The red damage effects coming off this arm were replaced with a yellow glow—a charged punch.

The attack it unleashed didn't hit Sally—but it left a *dent* where it hit the floor.

"Solid power buffs...but still too slow!"

Sally backed away, and the goblin gave chase, eyes bloodshot.

"You sure you wanna come after me? I bet *she's* way more terrifying."

"Hydra!"

Maple's voice summoned a three-headed dragon.

The goblin had been so busy chasing Sally that it had ignored the greater threat and left its back exposed to the Hydra's wrath.

The attack alone did massive damage—and it left the boss poisoned.

The fact that it remained standing at all was likely sheer doggedness.

But this did not last long. A moment later, its massive bulk exploded in a shower of light.

"Nice!"

"Very. So what's up with your mystery moves?"

"You mean Cover Move? It's the best! Turns out I was right. I can move *and* attack with it!"

"You're literally the only person who can use it like that and survive, much less *attack* with it..."

If any other great shielder even tried, they'd be downed in no time due to the doubled incoming damage.

Cover Move had been designed to allow players to momentarily expand the area they were defending. It was never intended to give someone the ability to warp around the room like Maple was.

And only Maple had an attack like Devour. A skill like that was the only way Cover Move could function offensively at all. Anything less would make the tactic not worthwhile.

And frankly, if the goal was to unleash that kind of DPS, why would anyone logically main a great shield?

"You're so fast, Sally! Especially at the end!"

"Yeah, that skill gives me a fifty percent AGI boost, so... But I gotta wait half an hour before I can use it again. Which is fine with me!"

Sally pulled up her status menu and showed Maple the skill description.

Superspeed

50% AGI boost. Lasts one minute. Thirty-minute cooldown.

Simple but powerful. And perfect for Sally's build.

"I've only got seven more uses left on Devour... I tried not to overuse it in a single fight, but..."

"You're not exactly fuel efficient. Let's make sure you pick a solid skill at the end of this event!"

"Yeah, good plan."

They headed for the goblin's throne.

There was a large, unadorned chest there.

"Do the honors?"

"Sure! Here goes!"

Sally flung it open.

Inside was a saber. Just like the goblin had used.

And two silver medals.

"Ooh! Medals!"

"And two of them! Double the reward!"

Both girls completely ignored the saber. Neither one of them could equip it, so naturally, it did not command their attention.

"If there are two medals in every dungeon...are there one hundred and fifty dungeons?"

"The number of medals likely changes depending on the

difficulty level. I bet there are way stronger bosses out there! And some medals might just be hidden, with no boss fights involved at all."

"Ahhh. Yeah, that makes sense."

Sally turned her attention to the saber, thinking they may as well check the description.

Goblin King Saber
[STR +75] [Fragile]

"Whoa…what a meathead weapon."

"Whatcha mean?"

"No durability, so you can't use it for long…but STR +75."

"But we can't equip it, right?"

"Nope."

"No luck with the equipment, huh?"

"It's fine—let's go find another dungeon. There's a magic circle behind the throne. That should take us outside."

"We should be able to clear another one today, right? I think my skills will last that long!"

They stepped into the magic circle.

Maple was limited to only ten uses of Devour a day, but conversely, that meant they wanted to explore long enough to use all ten if possible.

Any leftover uses couldn't be carried to the next day, so it was more efficient to tackle as many dungeons as they could.

When the light faded, they were back on the prairie.

"I almost forgot… Okay, first things first; we've gotta get out of all this grass."

"Wh-which way should we go?"

"Forward! Probably the shortest path. It can't possibly be grass all the way to those mountains, right?"

"I sure hope not!"

They turned their eyes to the peaks ahead and set out.

CHAPTER 2

Defense Build and Resuming Exploration

They spent a full hour walking across the grasslands.

At last, they spotted a forest ahead.

The change in scenery gave them a second wind, and they picked up the pace.

"W-we're finally here!"

"This is a big forest…"

They stepped into the trees.

It was a gloomy place. The branches above grew so thick that little light filtered through.

And with all these bushes, it was clearly designed for monster ambushes.

"I'll protect you!"

"No one could be more reliable."

If an attack could actually damage Maple, nobody else could survive it. There was no use worrying about monsters *that* strong. Sally kept her eyes peeled, walking one step behind Maple.

Thirty minutes later…

They'd yet to encounter a single ambush, and their search had proven entirely uneventful.

"Where are they?"

"At this point, the lack of ambushes is downright unsettling."

"Ah-ha-ha...yeah..."

The forest *was* eerily quiet.

The farther they went, the quieter it got.

"C-c'mon! Let's keep talking!" Sally squeaked, trying to keep her fears at bay.

"Eep? S-sure...um..."

Maple racked her brain for a topic, but as she did...

They heard a *foom* like a fire igniting.

This was the first new sound they'd heard in ages, and they both wheeled around to face it.

Behind them were several blue wisps floating in the air, wafting in their direction.

"It's just a game; it's just a game...! A game! Okay. I'm fine; I can do this...," Sally muttered.

"You don't sound fine!"

"Should we run? Let's run! I vote we run."

This proved Sally was *not* fine.

"Well, using Devour would be a waste, so..."

"Th-then take off your gear! I'll carry you... Aghhh, they're getting closer!"

With Maple's low AGI, Sally usually had to carry her if they wanted to move at anything approaching the same speed.

Removing her equipment made her lighter, but just in case, she kept New Moon out. Once she was ready, she climbed aboard the Sally Express.

Sally instantly sped off, like she couldn't stand staying another second.

Once the wisps appeared, other monsters started skulking about.

Floating skulls, multicolored wisps, zombies, suspiciously transparent people—all manner of ghosts and haunts.

"Ahhh! This forest was a mistake!"

"Wow! Such pretty fire! That one's green!"

The two girls' reactions were as disparate as the desert and the tundra, but they fled through the forest without fighting a single battle.

Eventually, they came upon a run-down house and temporarily took shelter within.

"This place is falling apart… Wanna look around?"

"Go right ahead."

"Hee-hee, you always were scared of ghosts."

"And I always will be. At least I'm fast enough in-game to get away from them… I didn't reach peak freak-out."

Sally sat down heavily on a nearby chair. Maple started poking around, but there wasn't much to poke.

There was pretty much nothing of note besides the remains of a table and the chair Sally occupied.

A filthy carpet under the table.

And an old chest of drawers.

No signs of a bed anywhere—clearly, nobody lived here.

There was still glass in the windows, but it was cracked or missing pieces.

"Anything in this chest…? Nope."

Maple has been hoping to find a medal, but evidently, it wasn't that easy.

She opened her status menu and checked the time.

"What do you think?" she asked. "In-game time, it's just past six. Almost night."

"Yeah... Maybe that's why the ghosts showed up. Ugh, our timing couldn't have been worse. We brought plenty of food with us, but I really don't wanna sleep *here*. On the other hand..."

Sally glanced nervously at the window.

There were shadows flitting past. Clearly not players. Maple took a look and confirmed those were definitely the zombies and ghosts they'd avoided on their way here.

If the monsters weren't breaking down the door, the ramshackle building must be a safe location.

Plus, if they went outside now, Sally would be plunged into a living hell.

"Well, it's better than nothing... This place'll have to do."

Maple stopped investigating the interior and returned to Sally. Since there was only one chair, she plopped down on the floor.

"Lemme put my gear back on, at least... I'll stick with White Snow for now. Should we play cards or something?"

Maple had several items for killing time in-game, including a set of cards.

"Maybe that would get my mind off things, but...no matter what game we play, it'd end pretty quickly with just two people."

"Oh! R-right, I didn't think of that...," Maple said sheepishly.

This finally made Sally crack a smile.

Feeling a little better, she took the cards from Maple's hand and started dealing.

The night had only just begun.

"Should be...this one!"

"Too bad! That's the joker."

"Hngg…," Maple groaned.

They'd gone from cards, to Othello, to chess, and back again.

The only break in between was to eat dinner.

Since they were inside a game, they didn't actually *have* to eat, but Sally insisted that it threw her rhythms off if she didn't get three meals a day and had brought a ton of provisions with her.

She'd given some to Maple, and they'd eaten together.

Maple, on the other hand, had mostly brought games.

"Hmm…this one? Ha! I win."

"Nooo!"

It was like they were on a school trip, except their lodging was a run-down shack deep inside a dark forest.

"Wow, the time really flies… It's already ten," Maple said. She'd spotted the system clock as she put the cards back in her inventory.

"They're still prowling out there, huh? I guess we'll have to sleep here."

"Probably for the best. I'm sure there's a medal or some gear out in these woods…but we can look for them in the morning. Hopefully, the monsters all vanish."

"Sorry. We can't explore because of me…"

"Don't worry about it! We'll just have to make it up tomorrow."

"Roger, roger!"

They got out their sleeping bags and spread them on the floor.

After saying good night, Maple lay down.

There was still a chance the monsters would attack, so they were taking shifts, sleeping two hours each.

And Sally had drawn first watch.

"It's awfully quiet…"

The only sound in the shack was Maple's breathing. Sally was sitting on the lone chair, on guard.

But no monsters attacked. Maybe there was no need to worry so much.

When it was almost midnight, she got up to wake Maple.

That was when she heard a low, distorted voice coming from somewhere near the table.

It was fading in and out, but definitely was not in her imagination.

"Aiiiieeee!"

Sally had been about to wake up Maple, but instead she fell on her.

Maple's defense meant she slept right through the impact, but the triple combo of the low voice, the clank of her amor bumping against the floor, and Sally's bloodcurdling scream woke her right up.

"What's wrong?"

"A—a ghost! Table! Table!"

Fear and panic had robbed Sally of most of her words. Maple decided to leave her to it and went to check on the table in question.

The voice was definitely coming from that vicinity.

Maple perked up her ears, trying to pin down the exact source.

"Is it...under the table?"

There was a ragged carpet on the floor.

Sally was curled up in a ball in the corner, so Maple was forced to move the table on her own.

This took a lot out of her. Her Strength stat was still at zero, after all.

Once it was finally out of the way, Maple peeled back the carpet.

"Oh...a basement entrance?"

There was a groove in the floor, with a handle attached.

Maple immediately yanked it open.

"That was easy! Hmm...there's a set of stairs."

The low voice had become much louder. It was definitely coming from down there.

"Should I check it out?"

"I...I'm coming, too. Can't have you dying on me..."

Sally forced herself to stand up and then immediately plastered herself to Maple's shadow.

"I'll guard your back!" she said.

"Thanks... All right! Let's do this."

Sally nodded emphatically, and they headed toward the source of the voice.

Down the basement stairs.

One stair at a time, on guard, down, down, down.

The voice grew steadily louder. Maple—taking the lead in case of surprise attacks—spotted an ancient door at the base of the staircase.

She reached for the doorknob.

"...It's not locked. I'll open it on your call."

"Gotcha. I'm good. Go for it."

Maple pushed the door open and hefted her shield. As the door swung open, the voice suddenly grew clear.

"It hurts...it huuuurts...aughhhh...ah..."

Maple peered around the edge of her great shield.

In the center of the floor was a half-melted candle.

That flickering light illuminated a blood-covered man, bound to a chair.

"He doesn't seem hostile... But that's definitely not a player."

Sally timidly peeked out from Maple's shadow and winced at the sight.

"What now?"

"Um…he says it hurts, so…we should heal him?"

"I know Heal. Should I try it?"

"Yeah…go for it!"

With that settled, Sally cast Heal.

The man was bathed in a gentle glow, and though he visibly recovered a bit, nearly all his wounds remained.

"Here's some more! Heal!"

Keeping a close eye on the man's condition, Sally cast the spell again and again.

She went through two MP potions before the man was finally fully healed.

The girls grinned at each other.

"Thank…you…," the man said, smiling. Then his body slowly faded out, changing to light and vanishing.

"Did he…pass on?"

"I guess? Didn't seem like he was alive to begin with. Hmm?"

Sally noticed something resting on the man's chair. It glimmered in the flickering candlelight.

She scooped it up.

"A ring?"

"Oh! He left us a reward?"

Sally checked the black ring's description.

Life Ring
[HP +100]

"Hmm. Seems like a better version of your Toughness Ring. Not bad considering how easy it was to obtain. Good for you anyway."

Sally passed the ring on.

"You can have it, Maple. Not much point in me boosting HP, and you're not planning on spending any points there, are you? Putting in a single point in HP or MP would give you twenty, which is pretty huge, but..."

Sally already knew what Maple's answer would be.

"I've made up my mind to spend all my points on VIT! But you're sure about the ring? It might be event-only!"

That got a grin out of Sally.

"If you're not comfortable just taking it off me, then let's say you owe me one. If you get any gear you don't need later in the event, you can pay me back with it."

"Makes sense! Let's go with that, then. I guess I'd better equip this baby right away."

Maple's total HP was doubled, clocking in at a big old 200.

This definitely gave her a much bigger safety buffer.

This also filled her last accessory slot, making it hard to raise her HP any further with items.

"Guess we should go back to sleep..."

Sleeping in-game helped recover a player's ability to focus, and Sally's life depended on that, so she needed to get *some* sleep. Though it was possible to keep playing even without sleep, her performance would definitely suffer for it.

"Think this is all this forest has to offer?"

"Hmm...hard to say. I feel like there oughtta be at least one more thing, but...time of day seems to be a factor. This one was only active 'cause it was midnight, right?"

If there was anything else around, it could very well be time-sensitive paranormal activity, which meant they could spend days stuck here without any guarantee they'd find anything.

"Then we should probably ditch this forest tomorrow."

"Yeah, I agree."

Sally was against spending time in a haunted forest to begin with.

The two girls went back up the stairs, moved the table to its previous place, and returned to their original sleep schedule.

"Good night, Maple."

"Good night! I'll keep close watch. Never fear!"

"Heh-heh…thanks."

And thus, they whiled the night away.

The second day had arrived.

"Let's make it a good one!"

"Mm!"

As soon as they finished breakfast, it was time to set out.

To minimize the time spent in the forest, Sally was carrying Maple.

Every now and then, they stopped so Sally could climb a tree and check their heading.

It was still a good hour before they reached the other side.

"Woo! Freedom!"

"Hngg! It's been so long since we got any real sunlight…I can barely make out anything."

Maple put her equipment back on and stretched.

Before them was a wasteland. Barely anything grew here besides a couple of patchy scraps of grass and a few trees so dried out, they looked ready to crumble at the slightest breeze. It seemed to stretch all the way to the mountains in the distance.

"Guess we keep heading that way? They don't seem to be getting much closer."

Maple didn't really have any other destinations in mind, so she readily agreed.

"You really don't get biome transitions this abrupt outside of games…"

"It's always exciting having no clue what's in the next zone, though!"

They forged ahead, chatting away. This wasteland left no room to hide, and it was easy to spot monsters coming.

It also made it easy to spot the trio of players in the distance.

"People up front, Maple."

"How's their gear? Should I have Devour ready?"

"Might need it, yeah. If they're looking to fight…we can get you in range with Cover Move. Also…"

Sally whispered a plan in Maple's ear.

"Roger that!"

On guard, the two moved closer. Maple had come in third in the last event, so most players recognized her.

And some of them might want to steal her gold medal.

The other party saw them approaching and stopped, huddling up to confer.

Then they approached to meet Maple and Sally. Nobody drew their weapons.

All three players were male. A greatsword, a dagger, and a one-handed sword.

When they were within earshot, one called out, "First time seeing anyone, and we draw a top player…"

"Yeah, this is wild. We're not looking for a fight! Mind letting us pass in peace…?"

"The three of us are just headed for those mountains. We'd rather not waste any skills if we can help it."

"Gotcha," Maple said. "We're going the same way. Feels like those peaks have gotta be hiding something, after all…"

They all nodded, then suggested they travel together.

"What do you think, Sally?"

"………I guess it'll probably be fine."

And so the five of them set off together.

"Then I'll take the lead. Maple, stand in front of those three and guard 'em."

"Got it! No matter what monsters come, nothing can get past me!"

Maple raised her great shield.

"That's a confidence booster."

"Totally."

They walked on, ignoring the muttering from the rear.

A number of monsters attacked, but Maple's protection was never needed—Sally took care of everything.

Finally, their destination drew near.

"Phew! Just a little farther!" Maple said, stretching.

Then…

"Now! Armor Crusher!"

"Defense Break!"

"Piercing Blade!"

The three men behind her all attacked at once.

Every skill they used ignored defense.

They'd been waiting the whole time for their chance to strike. It was the perfect surprise attack.

"Cover Move!"

But their blades never touched Maple.

Sally's plan had involved letting these three come with them, and Maple had deliberately given them an opening to test their real intentions.

Sally had agreed to the team-up well aware that they might be planning this attack.

As long as Sally was in range, Maple could easily speed away.

Her safety wasn't exactly guaranteed, but Maple had agreed to Sally's scheme anyway.

And paid close attention to the other party's movements.

They hadn't noticed she was watching them.

The three of them were too busy stalking their prey to realize she was already stalking them.

"Wha—?!"

Shocked by the failure of their ambush, the attackers froze.

They'd been so certain.

"Hydra!"

And Maple's counterattack swallowed them up, melting their health bars.

"They really did attack…"

"Well, they've got good reason to be after you, Maple. Good thing we were cautious, right?"

"Yeah, I was ready to activate Cover Move right away. Might have been cutting it a little close otherwise…"

"Now…time to see if they had any medals. They might have dropped some."

Maple waded out into the lake of poison. She checked the ground where their attackers had fallen but found nothing.

"Guess there's no easy path to riches."

"Yeah, seems like it."

Maple and Sally had scored a quick victory in their first PVP encounter of the event.

"Welp, let's change gears and scale this mountain!"

"Let's do it!"

They headed on up the slope.

The incline was getting steeper.

They were definitely in the mountains now. At first, the foothills didn't seem much different from the wasteland, but now there was snow around them, and the ground was getting slippery.

"There's snow everywhere, but it isn't cold at all. So strange."

"Yeah," Sally said. "But if it was cold, climbing a mountain would be totally impossible in this gear, so I'm glad."

They pressed on.

"Let's assume other players set their sights on this mountain, too. It would be a drag if we fell behind."

"Yeah, let's try to hurry."

They picked up the pace, continuing toward the highest peak. At the moment, there were no other players in sight.

But there was a strong possibility someone was climbing up the other side. No telling when they'd bump into other people.

"Maple! Monsters coming!"

"I see 'em!"

Maple switched her shield to White Snow.

There was likely a boss up here somewhere, so she wanted to keep Devour in reserve.

The forest may have been largely combat-free, but there were a lot of monsters on the mountain itself, and they'd been fighting a lot.

"Nice, a level-up! Level nineteen! Let's spend…everything on Agility!"

There were big rocks scattered around, perfect for monster ambushes. They couldn't let their guard down for a second.

They kept their eyes peeled, moving forward and fending off attacks whenever they occurred.

When bird monsters swooped toward them, their only option was to rely on Sally's magic—which meant she was burning through MP.

Their main enemies on the ground were very agile wolves.

"The footing's so poor, it makes these fights extra tough."

"The faster we get up this thing, the better!"

With all the combat, it took them two and a half hours to make any headway.

Now snow was piled high all around. Every step they took made a crunching sound.

"We've come pretty far."

"Yeah, but looks like we're still at least an hour from the peak," Sally commented, peering up at it.

As she did, she spotted a monster.

A white-furred monkey, twenty yards uphill.

It charged toward them, snow flying in its wake.

"Incoming!"

"Yup!"

As they braced themselves, two bluish-white magic circles appeared beside it.

This was clearly not your average critter.

It was casting magic.

"Cover!" Maple jumped to guard Sally.

A string of blows bounced off her great shield.

It was like a machine gun had shot chunks of ice instead of bullets. But Maple stood her ground.

The monkey kept closing in. The circles vanished, and it came swinging, a white glow enveloping its fist.

Maple blocked with her shield. This impact was even stronger.

"Sally!"

"Double Slash!"

While Maple had the monkey occupied, Sally slipped past it, slashing its back.

The monster screamed but was not so easily defeated. It spun toward Sally, eyes filled with fury, and swung a fist at her.

The snow made it hard to dart around, but Sally had no trouble evading this blow.

"Power Attack!"

She countered with two heavy strikes to the monkey's gut—but it was *still* standing.

The monkey's jaw yawned open, and a glittering white magic circle appeared within.

Sally didn't hesitate to pull out her trump card.

"Superspeed!"

She dodged, and an instant later, the space she'd vacated was pulverized by jagged shards of ice.

"Slash!"

Her counterblow finally slayed the monkey.

Its body turned to light and vanished.

"Whew… That thing actually made me resort to Superspeed."

"Maybe I should be doing more?"

"No, we wanna keep you rested up for the boss fight. Superspeed'll be ready again by then, so…I'll handle the fodder along the way!"

"Hmm…well, that sounds like a plan. But I'm gonna keep using Cover."

"Thanks! It definitely helps."

They pressed on through the snow. It was possible the monkey had been a mid-boss; they didn't encounter anything else like it.

Instead, they were fighting packs of moles that sent up white clouds with their serpentine movements and albino armadillos that came rolling along, plowing through the snowfields.

"Gotta be careful around the moles, but as long as you dodge the armadillos, they just roll away. No problem."

"But if they hit you, you'll probably die instantly. Well…not *you*, Maple."

They resumed their climb…

And at last they reached the peak.

At the top of the mountain was a circular clearing with a stone shrine at the center.

A white magic circle lay in front of the shrine, glittering invitingly.

Clearly, a transport spell.

They walked toward it.

At the same time, four players entered the clearing from the other side.

A party of two mages, a greatsworder, and a great shielder.

They saw the girls coming.

Sally braced for PVP—but that didn't happen.

"Oh, Chrome!"

"Mm? Maple! Didn't think I'd see you here. Uh, we'd rather not fight. I doubt we could win…"

Chrome's party put their weapons away and held up their hands.

"We don't wanna fight, either. Right, Sally?"

"Yeah, sure. No use wasting resources if we don't have to. Let's stay ready for anything, but…you think we can trust them, right?"

Who could really trust anybody completely under these circumstances? Sally kept her guard up.

"So… What do we do about this shrine?" Sally said. "Only one party can claim the reward."

This was a fair point. One of their parties would have to go in first, and if they cleared the dungeon inside, there might not be any rewards left.

Maple thought about this for a while.

"Hmm…Sally, mind if we give Chrome's party first dibs?" she said, clasping her hands together.

Sally was certainly surprised by this, but she soon grinned back.

"If you wanna play it that way, I'm cool with it," she said. "Just promise me you won't regret it later."

"I won't!" Maple promised. "All right, Chrome! Go on in."

"Y-you're sure? These things are usually finders keepers…"

"I'm sure! Get on in there before I change my mind."

Chrome's party gave their thanks, stepped into the magic circle, and was gone. The circle's glow vanished.

The two girls waited, alone on the mountaintop.

"That was for the best, right?"

"Yeah…if we fought here, we'd end up wasting skills, and then we'd probably run into trouble in the dungeon. Plus, I don't wanna fight friends."

"Fair enough. Nothing to regret… Also, they oughtta be in combat by now, huh?" Sally glanced at the faded circle.

"Probably."

"What now? Head back down? They might not win…and since we *did* save up our skills, we could wait and see."

No sooner had the words left her mouth than the circle started gleaming.

Allowing entry once more.

""Huh?""

This surprised them both.

It had been less than a minute since Chrome's party went in.

That was way too fast.

"Wh-what do you think?" Maple said.

Sally thought it over. "I can think of two explanations," she said. "First, this is one of those places that has nothing besides a chest with medals or gear, and all you have to do is open it. Second…"

She paused, scowling. Clearly, she didn't like the second possibility.

"…the monster inside is so strong, they were wiped right away."

"Yikes."

"I'm thinking it's the latter, too. If the circle's glowing again, that means the challenge is still open. So whatever's inside—wasn't just a chest. Probably."

Didn't look like any more players were on their way, so they took some time to check their stats and strategize.

* * *

"Destructive Growth means my armor is now VIT +40, and my HP's higher, too. And I haven't used my limited skills at all yet."

"Mine haven't changed much, either. Superspeed's recharged, and I haven't used Mirage yet today."

Maple

Lv24   HP 40/40 <+160>   MP 12/12 <+10>

[STR 0]   [VIT 170 <+81>]
[AGI 0]   [DEX 0]
[INT 0]

Equipment

Head	[None]	Body	[Black Rose Armor]
R. Hand	[New Moon: Hydra]	L. Hand	[Night's Facsimile: Devour]
Legs	[Black Rose Armor]	Feet	[Black Rose Armor]
Accessories	[Forest Queen Bee Ring]		
	[Toughness Ring]		
	[Life Ring]		

Skills

Shield Attack, Sidestep, Deflect, Meditation, Taunt
HP Boost (S), MP Boost (S)
Great Shield Mastery IV, Cover Move I, Cover
Absolute Defense, Moral Turpitude, Giant Killing, Hydra Eater, Bomb Eater

Sally

Lv19 HP 32/32 MP 25/25 <+35>

[STR 25 <+20>] [VIT 0]
[AGI 80 <+68>] [DEX 25 <+20>]
[INT 25 <+20>]

Equipment

Head	[Surface Scarf: Mirage]	Body	[Oceanic Coat: Oceanic]
R. Hand	[Deep Sea Dagger]	L. Hand	[Seabed Dagger]
Legs	[Oceanic Clothes]	Feet	[Black Boots]
Accessories	[None]		
	[None]		
	[None]		

Skills

Slash, Double Slash, Gale Slash, Defense Break
Down Attack, Power Attack, Switch Attack
Fire Ball, Water Ball, Wind Cutter
Sand Cutter, Dark Ball
Water Wall, Wind Wall, Refresh, Heal
Affliction III
Strength Boost (S), Combo Boost (S), Martial Arts I
MP Boost (S), MP Cost Down (S), MP Recovery Speed
Boost (S), Poison Resist (S)
Gathering Speed Boost (S)
Dagger Mastery II, Magic Mastery II

Fire Magic I, Water Magic II, Wind Magic II
Earth Magic I, Dark Magic I, Light Magic II
Presence Block II, Presence Detect II, Sneaky Steps I,
Leap I
Fishing, Swimming X, Diving X, Cooking I, Jack of All
Trades, Superspeed

"I guess I'll put my shield up the second we step in. You should take cover behind me."

"Got it. After that…"

They hashed out their plan for a good twenty minutes before finally stepping onto the circle.

"Right! Here goes nothing!"

"Brace yourself!"

The circle activated, their bodies were wreathed in light—and they vanished.

CHAPTER 3

Defense Build and the Transport Destination

Once the light around them faded, they could see clearly again.

Maple raised her great shield, wary of surprise attacks. But the powerful opening attack they'd feared never arrived.

In fact, there were no signs of any monsters.

The girls scanned their surroundings cautiously.

They found themselves in a large circular space.

There were glowing blue crystals set in the walls and no ceiling at all.

Snow was falling.

"Chrome's party...is already gone."

"Probably respawned at their starting point. But...that fast?"

Wariness rising, Sally searched for clues.

On the far wall was an extra-large crystal formation—and a giant bird's nest on top of it.

The nest was unoccupied—for now. The silence was heavy.

"Okay...I think I get it. The boss here's gonna be a giant bird. Oceanic may not help much..."

Oceanic was one of Sally's skills. It lowered enemy AGI, but since the effect spread outward from her feet, it was unlikely to hit a flying enemy.

"What do we do? Approach the nest?"

"...Carefully. It'll most likely show itself the moment we do."

Watching each other's backs, they inched toward the nest.

And when they were five yards from it...

A deafening roar exploded overhead, and something plunged down out of the sky.

The girls had been expecting this and were able—barely—to leap backward, out of the way.

A jagged pillar of ice smashed into the spot they had been standing in just moments earlier.

It was followed by a monstrous bird with wings the color of snow.

There was a piercing gleam in its eyes, every bit as sharp as its beak and talons. Its entire form radiated power.

Diplomacy was clearly not an option.

The fight had already begun.

Magic circles appeared on either side of the bird.

These launched so many ice chunks that nothing could be seen behind the incoming fusillade.

"Cover!"

Maple lowered her shield and planted herself in front of Sally.

If she blocked this volley the normal way, she'd lose all uses of Devour at once.

"Good! It's not piercing!"

Any chunks that hit Maple's body were rendered powerless.

This bird seemed to be a good deal smarter than your average monster. It quickly realized the attack wasn't working, merged the magic circles together, and fired the same massive ice spike it had used to open the fight.

What it gained in power, it lost in coverage.

Sally spotted an opening and darted out.

"Maple!"

"Cover Move!"

Maple forcibly caught up with Sally when she was a few yards from the bird.

They were only a couple of steps away when it let out an ear-splitting shriek.

A white magic circle appeared, covering the entire floor.

"Crap…!"

There was a rumble, and massive spikes of ice shot out of the ground, each over a yard tall.

They covered every inch of the ground…except the area around Maple.

The cloud of snow and ice scattered—revealing Maple, with her shield pointed at the ground.

"…………Whew, glad you thought of that, Maple!"

"Only six Devour left!"

"Roger that!"

Sally kicked off a spike, leaping toward the bird.

The footholds were so bad, she couldn't afford to stop for even a second.

The bird tried to slash her with its claws, moving every bit as fast as she was.

"Superspeed!"

The bird took a moment to react to her sudden acceleration. And in the dizzying chaos of battle, that proved fatal.

"Cover Move!"

Maple closed the distance instantly, putting her great shield between Sally and the talons—and swallowing up the bird's entire leg.

The monster raised a howl of pain and anger.

And that gave Maple time to attack again.

"Hydra!"

A three-headed dragon swallowed the giant bird.

Maple landed on the poison-coated ice spikes below while Sally leaped away, observing the results.

The bird let out a wave of extreme cold that froze the poison coating it.

Then that frozen poison shattered, scattering the glittering shards onto the ground.

"That only took out ten percent of its HP?!"

"You're kidding!"

They'd been expecting Maple's attacks to end this fight quickly, but this thing was clearly a damage sponge.

While they gaped, the ice spikes around the bird lifted off the ground, breaking and gathering together...

And a few seconds later, the ice missiles shot forward.

"Cover Move! Cover!"

Maple jumped in front of Sally, lowering her shield and taking the hits head-on.

Red damage effects sprayed all over her.

"Agh! It's getting through! Meditation!"

Cover Move's side effect meant piercing damage was doubled. Each shot that hit her was taking 10 percent off Maple's health bar. It was dropping *fast*.

"Heal!"

Their strategy for unavoidable piercing damage was to have

Maple activate Meditation and recover over time, while Sally stood behind her casting Heal as fast as she could.

The best they could do was keep this up until the volley slowed down.

The barrage lasted a good twenty seconds.

When the ice stopped pounding around them, the surrounding area was torn to pieces.

"Time to move!"

"Yup!"

They ran off in opposite directions.

The bird targeted Sally and hurtled after her.

"Focus!" she yelled, whipping her mind into action. Her eyes locked on the boss.

There were ice chunks flying alongside it.

But because the bird was flying with them, the gaps were much wider.

And at max focus, Sally could slip in between those.

"Leap!"

Timing her jump flawlessly, she sailed over the top of the bird.

"Slash!"

And as she passed over it, she sliced its back—not forgetting to use her Affliction skill to apply a paralysis effect.

The more paralysis she stacked on it, the more openings to attack they'd have.

The actual damage she'd done was so small, it wasn't even visible to the naked eye, but that didn't mean it was *nothing*.

The bird wheeled around, spread its wings, and flapped them hard.

The resulting gale violently uprooted the remaining spikes, creating a hail of ice that was hard to predict.

Sally used Leap again, throwing herself sideways, out of the gale's path.

"Hydra!" Maple yelled. With Sally out of the way, the dragon had a clear path to the bird again.

Since it had just finished furiously flapping, the bird was unable to react to Maple's attack in time.

One of the three dragon heads struck home.

"Wind Cutter! Fire Ball!"

Sally was throwing out attacks every chance she got, just trying to chip away whatever health she could.

Once again, the poison froze and was shaken off.

The bird must have registered Hydra as a serious threat, because this time it charged at Maple.

But the ice chunks couldn't damage her, so that posed no problem.

She didn't even try to dodge.

The bird swung its talons at Maple, attempting to rip her in two.

Maple raised her great shield, trying to swallow the bird whole.

The bird reeled backward, spewing damage effects everywhere.

Seizing the chance, Maple swung her shield again.

There were red sparks skittering off her body, too.

The bird's damage output was so high that even without a piercing effect, it could overwhelm Maple's 1,000+ points of Vitality.

But it was obvious at a glance which side had come out worse from the exchange.

The HP bar floating over the bird was down to 70 percent.

"Leap!"

As the bird staggered back, Sally vaulted onto its back again.

"Oceanic!"

A burst of water spread out across the bird's back.

The bird's body was drenched.

It let out a roar and thrashed wildly, but Sally had already leaped away.

The boss was moving noticeably slower.

"Hydra!"

And at this range, without its full speed, there was no way it could dodge.

Its health took another solid hit.

"Double Slash! Fire Ball!"

Maple was wrecking its HP from up close.

Meanwhile, Sally was mounting hit-and-run attacks, stacking paralysis effects whenever she could.

And Maple's great shield swallowed another chunk of bird boss.

The bird's talons had Maple down to half health, but that was far from fatal.

But when the bird's HP hit the halfway point…

It suddenly backed away, sinking its talons deep into the ground.

Its beak yawned open, and the magic circle it revealed was twice Maple's height.

Both knew instantly—this was *bad*.

"Cover Move! Cover!"

Just as the words left Maple's lips…

Silver laser beams blanketed everything in sight.

Several seconds later, the blinding light faded.

The terrain around them was in ruins. A testament to the sheer power of the laser beam attack.

Maple was standing at the center of those ruins, shield held high.

This stalwart defense had allowed Sally to escape the lasers of death.

Sally used Heal to replenish Maple's HP.

Still taking cover in Maple's shadow, she drank a potion, recharging her MP.

"One more Devour."

"Yeah, I know."

There was no way to withstand those lasers without Devour.

They'd survived the attack, but at the cost of using up their main damage dealer.

The scales were tipping against them.

"If it uses those lasers again, Cover Move me," Sally said, talking quickly. "Stay close."

Then she ran off toward the bird. Maple followed closely.

With its attention focused on Sally, she could slip in another Hydra attack.

The bird raked the ground with its talons, fluttered into the air, and started spamming ice chunks again.

All aimed at Sally.

Maple may have easily blocked these, but Sally knew...

If one so much as nicked her, she was done for.

Like her battle against the giant fish, her concentration went into overdrive.

The chunks seemed to slow—and she could spot the gaps between them now.

Sally's body twisted, slipping between them.

She crouched, jumped, even smashed some with her weapons—until she was right up against the bird.

"Double Slash!"

She dodged ice chunks and talons, mixing up her skills and stringing attacks together relentlessly.

The boss tried to use its claws to take her out, but each time, Sally escaped by a hairbreadth.

And each time it swung, she cut at another spot on its legs.

"Slash!"

Each cut was tiny.

But the more paralysis she stacked, the less the bird could move.

"Hydra!"

Sally had risked her life to create this opportunity, and Maple didn't waste it.

The bird's movements had become far too sluggish to avoid the poison dragon.

Sally had done everything she could to maximize Maple's chances.

And Maple held up her end.

The bird's health bar was now just over 40 percent.

"Venom Cutter!" Maple yelled, attacking again. A magic circle appeared at the tip of her blade—nowhere near as strong as Hydra, but damage was damage.

Sally was hurling spells at it, too, chipping away.

When the boss's health dipped below 40 percent, the paralysis wore off, and it was free again.

It targeted Maple this time, spamming the hail-laden gale attack.

This attack couldn't hurt Maple, so she lowered her shield, saving her last Devour.

While the ice was pelting Maple, Sally was free to attack in relative safety.

Her rush took off another 5 percent.

But doing damage at these speeds burned through her MP.

She had to keep a close eye on it or she'd be tapped out right when she needed it most.

The moment the boss hit 35 percent health…

The bird stopped sending out gales and took off.

Both girls figured that meant nothing good. They huddled together in the center of the room.

Peering up through the falling snow, they could see the bird's glittering white wings turning black, as if darkness were swallowing them whole.

The bird boss's HP bar started draining—and kept draining, until it had only 10 percent left.

The bird's scream shook the very air.

"Here it comes!"

"I noticed!"

Maple raised her shield, ready to sacrifice her last Devour.

The pitch-black bird folded its wings, diving toward them.

It hit Maple's shield at supersonic speeds.

Her last Devour swallowed half its remaining HP but left Maple's great shield without its strongest means of protecting her.

A swift strike from the bird's talons…

And the great shield snapped in two.

Her armor had been rent asunder.

*　　*　　*

Her HP dropped below 10 percent.

"Unh…aghhh…!"
It dealt so much damage, she gasped aloud. Dark light poured from the bird's mouth.

"Maple!"
Sally leaped into the air.
Maple's best chance at survival came because the wheels in Sally's brain never once stopped turning.
"Cover Move!"
This desperate cry sent her rocketing toward Sally's position, narrowly avoiding the laser beams.
The bird turned to charge again.
Its speed was downright unreasonable, way beyond even Sally's estimations.
But before the attack hit her…
"Cover!"
Maple stepped between them.
She had less than 10 percent health but chose to protect Sally, knowing full well it might be the last action she could take.
Maple didn't think about it much. Her body moved on sheer instinct.

Her great shield and armor were stronger now, thanks to Destructive Growth—but the bird's claws tore through Maple anyway.

Damage effects sprayed everywhere.

But Maple did *not* die.

When her HP bar had only the slimmest of lines left, a white halo appeared around her body.

"Leap!"

The claw attack had left the bird's limb fully extended, and Sally knew this was their last chance. She had no idea how Maple had survived, but she pushed all speculation out of her mind, throwing herself at the bird.

Maple warped after her.

A purple magic circle gleamed at the end of her short sword.

That last attack had left the bird off-balance—it had no way to dodge.

Sally was certain they'd won.

But the bird's eyes took on a sinister gleam, and a pitch-black magic circle appeared between them. Sally realized victory was merely an illusion.

Surprise and fear showed on both girls' faces, but they were in midair, and there was nothing they could do.

Before Hydra could activate, the bird's spell showered them in magic missiles.

The bird's final trump card swallowed the girls.

Both of them disappeared in the hail of shots.

It was like they'd never been there.

"How d'ya like *that* trick?"

An instant after the barrage ended, the air shimmered—and Sally appeared.

All this time...

She'd been saving Mirage for this exact moment.

Since she hadn't used it yet, the bird had no way of preparing for it.

"Cover Move!"

The real Maple caught up to Sally.

They were at point-blank range. Too close for the bird to dodge.

"Hydra!"

The poison engulfed it.

Its tail thrashed. It screamed.

And it sank to the ground.

White light poured out of its body, showering over the girls like a blessing from above.

"We did it...we won..."

"I'm so tired... Can I just sleep right here?"

Feeling absolutely ragged, they collapsed to the floor.

"Oh, right. What was *that* skill? How'd you survive that last attack?"

"Hang on...looks like it's called Indomitable Guardian. Great-shielder skill obtained by protecting an ally at less than ten percent health. Can only be used once a day but lets you survive a fatal hit with one HP."

"Oh, makes sense. I've heard of skills like that before. I think all I got was a level-up... Wait, that means you only have one HP?! Heal!"

Warm light enveloped Maple, and her HP was restored.

Much less risk of surprise death.

They stood up, ready to check for spoils.

"The bird died in a lake of poison, so you'd better do the honors."

"Sure. Where are you going?"

"I'm gonna go check out that nest!"

They split up and headed in opposite directions.

There was no sign of any chests, but there had to be *some* sort of reward in here.

Maple went sloshing through the poison, searching the ground where the bird had died.

"Oh! It did drop some materials!" she called.

Four black claws—strong enough they'd even hurt Maple. And three white feathers.

Clearly all top-tier materials.

"Maple! Come here!" Sally called, peering over the edge.

Maple ran up, standing right below the nest.

"Is the coast clear?"

"Yup! Cover Move it."

"Gotcha! Cover Move!"

She kicked the wall, launched herself into the air, and zipped to Sally's side. In the nest were two eggs and five medals.

"Monster bird eggs?"

"No, they're different colors and sizes. The bird might have stolen them from somewhere. No telling what'll hatch."

"Should we take them with us?"

"Definitely. It asked if I wanted to stick them in my inventory, so…which one do you want?"

"You don't mind me picking?"

"Not at all. The choice is yours!"

One egg had a dark-green shell. The other was a light purple.

"Then…I like green better, so I'll take this one!"

"That makes this one mine."

They both checked the eggs' descriptions.

Monster Egg

Will hatch if kept warm.

"Not enough info!"

"I thought the same thing. Why would I wanna hatch a monster? Maybe we can tame them...?"

This game didn't have summoner or tamer classes, so the odds weren't high, but given how ridiculously strong the bird boss had been, there was a chance it was a unique reward.

They decided to keep the eggs and see.

They each took two talons, and since Maple had been given first dibs on the eggs, Sally got the extra feather.

They hopped down from the nest, heading for the exit circle.

"Wait, there are three of them?"

Like Maple said, there were three magic circles.

It seemed safe to assume each led to a different location.

"Sally, thoughts?"

"You're out of Devour, so I'd rather go someplace combat-free..."

Pondering the problem, Sally paced back and forth a minute. Then she stopped next to one of the circles.

"Let's pick this one!"

"Cool! Here we go!"

They stepped onto the circle and vanished in a burst of light.

All that remained of their epic battle were the scars on the room itself.

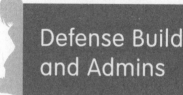

Defense Build
and Admins

Inside the accelerated game, in a zone no player could reach...

The game admins were monitoring the event, on the lookout for any bugs.

A horrified shriek echoed across the room.

"Aaaaaaaaaaaauuughhh! Silver Wings died!"

Everyone turned to stare at him.

"Huh? Silver Wings? But that was designed to be unbeatable!"

"Yeah, it was jammed full of high-DPS skills, ridiculous HP and MP, high stats across the board. The thing's basically an embodiment of our spite."

"Who took it out?!"

"Pulling up the feed..."

He fiddled with the controls and put the video on-screen.

A giant bird with glittering white wings.

Facing a girl in black armor and a girl in blue.

"*Maple*?! Seriously?! Even *she* shouldn't stand a chance against Silver Wings, though!"

"She's not mobile enough! I could see her taking on the earth dragon, but…"

But even as they denied it, the battle was unfolding before their eyes.

"Those chunks aren't… Well, I guess we should've seen that coming."

"Her defense is too broken."

The admins were all keeping one eye on their main work and the other on the screen.

They very quickly discovered the problem.

"I see what's going on! The blue girl *is* Maple's mobility!"

On-screen, Maple was warping around the map with Cover Move.

They had not expected this.

All eyes were on-screen now.

"Her name's Sally. AGI focused, lots of skills, but nothing super developed yet. Only really powerful skills are Mirage and Oceanic."

One admin had pulled up Sally's stats.

"She's pretty normal, really? I mean, anyone would be, compared to Maple."

"You can say that again."

An awkward chuckle went around the room.

But it was soon clear how abnormal Sally was.

"…I take it back. She's *nuts*. Maybe even more broken than Maple."

"She doesn't have precog skills, right?!"

"Nope, not a one."

On-screen, Sally was avoiding Silver Wings's attacks like no human ever could.

Moving like she had psychic powers telling her where the next attack would be.

"How is she *doing* that?!"

"I couldn't slip through that gap if I stopped *time*!"

They watched the rest of the fight in stunned horror.

Then someone gasped.

"Crap! They've taken the Mythical Eggs!"

"What's in them?"

"A fox and a turtle. Not...the worst..."

"The bird and the wolf are...?"

"With the Sea Emperor. It's set so those only spawn there... They should be fine..."

"You'd absolutely need some fancy tricks to have any chance of getting those." Someone sighed, slumping back in their chair. "Ugh...I can't believe it. And *after* we nerfed her!"

"Anyone with a second to spare, double-check all the medal exchange skills! Anything that seems remotely open to abuse!"

""On it!""

"..............Why don't we just make *them* the last boss?"

"Yeah...she kinda already is..."

Their voices sounded exhausted.

But of course, Maple and Sally would never know this conversation had taken place.

CHAPTER 4

Defense Build and Late-Night Exploration

The girls emerged from the transport circle.

She was out of Devour, but Maple still had her shield braced for surprise attacks.

"I think we're good?"

They checked their surroundings.

The teleportation had brought them to the center of a ruined town. The remains of fallen buildings were everywhere.

Based on the location of the mountain peak, this was in the opposite direction from their original starting location.

"I guess we picked a good one?"

"But someone else might have already cleaned out this place."

"It's only day two. I bet there's still plenty of hidden stuff around. That said, this town's probably empty by now. I mean, the circle brought us here."

It seemed highly unlikely that the admins would just dump players on top of more medals right away.

Deciding to start exploring while keeping an eye out for a safe zone, they began investigating the ruins.

"Three players up ahead. What do you think?"

"I'd rather not fight. No Devour and…a loss would hurt."

"I agree. Let's go this way."

They discreetly slipped out of the ruins, entering a nearby forest.

There they found lots of spiders and owls.

After that bird boss, every other monster seemed like a joke.

So slow! So little damage! Such low HP!

"Easy peasy."

They pressed on. Looking for a safe place to spend the second night. Scaling the mountain had taken so long, the sun was already starting to set.

Stopping only to fight monsters, they moved deeper into the woods.

"Hmm… We still haven't found anything…"

Like Maple said, there was nothing here but trees. No buildings, no caves, nothing remarkable at all.

"Let's find a tall tree and climb it. That'll be better than the ground, at least."

Sally looked around for a tree with a good view and used her Leap skill to reach the top.

"Cover Move!"

Maple followed her up.

This tree had few low-hanging branches, so not many players would even consider climbing it.

They leaned against the trunk, taking a breather.

The fatigue of the bird fight had caught up with them.

"Sally…my Devour restocks at midnight. Are you thinking what I'm thinking?"

Maple was suggesting they should rest until their skills refreshed and then do some exploring at night.

The last romp in the forest had proved there were time-sensitive events out there.

Their goal was twenty medals.

That wasn't happening without some creativity and exploring as much as they could.

Plus, this was a race against the other players, to boot.

Dawdling now and panicking in the latter half would do them no good.

"If you're up for it, Maple."

"Mm, okay. Then let's kick things off at midnight!"

They'd both leveled up, so it was time to spend some skill points.

"I guess...AGI and STR?"

"All VIT!"

Maple

Lv26   HP 40/40 <+160>   MP 12/12 <+10>

[STR 0]   [VIT 175 <+141>]
[AGI 0]   [DEX 0]
[INT 0]

Equipment

Head	[None]	Body	[Black Rose Armor]
R. Hand	[New Moon: Hydra]	L. Hand	[Night's Facsimile: Devour]
Legs	[Black Rose Armor]	Feet	[Black Rose Armor]
Accessories	[Forest Queen Bee Ring]		
	[Toughness Ring]		
	[Life Ring]		

Skills

Shield Attack, Sidestep, Deflect, Meditation, Taunt
HP Boost (S), MP Boost (S)
Great Shield Mastery IV, Cover Move I, Cover
Absolute Defense, Moral Turpitude, Giant Killing, Hydra
Eater, Bomb Eater, Indomitable Guardian

Sally

Lv21   HP 32/32   MP 25/25 <+35>

[STR 30 <+20>]   [VIT 0]
[AGI 85 <+68>]   [DEX 25 <+20>]
[INT 25 <+20>]

Equipment

Head	[Surface Scarf: Mirage]	Body	[Oceanic Coat: Oceanic]
R. Hand	[Deep Sea Dagger]	L. Hand	[Seabed Dagger]
Legs	[Oceanic Clothes]	Feet	[Black Boots]
Accessories	[None]		
	[None]		
	[None]		

Skills

Slash, Double Slash, Gale Slash, Defense Break
Down Attack, Power Attack, Switch Attack
Fire Ball, Water Ball, Wind Cutter

Sand Cutter, Dark Ball
Water Wall, Wind Wall, Refresh, Heal
Affliction III
Strength Boost (S), Combo Boost (S), Martial Arts I
MP Boost (S), MP Cost Down (S), MP Recovery Speed
Boost (S), Poison Resist (S)
Gathering Speed Boost (S)
Dagger Mastery II, Magic Mastery II
Fire Magic I, Water Magic II, Wind Magic II
Earth Magic I, Dark Magic I, Light Magic II
Presence Block II, Presence Detect II, Sneaky Steps I,
Leap I
Fishing, Swimming X, Diving X, Cooking I, Jack of All
Trades, Superspeed

Maple had put five more points in Vitality, but Destructive Growth had added a full sixty.

And she had a new skill, Indomitable Guardian.

Sally put five points in Agility and five in Strength.

She handed Maple some food, and they both ate.

They had to rest as much as they could before midnight.

By the time they left the tree, it was so late that even most monsters had stopped prowling.

Her stock of Devour was back, and Maple was ready for anything.

This meant she'd swapped her shield back to White Snow. That was the easiest way to avoid wasting any uses.

"This forest? Or back to those ruins?"

"Uh...let's stick with the forest. There were other players in those ruins, so they've probably cleaned the place out already."

"Fair. Forest it is!"

They plunged deeper into the woods.

Every now and then, an owl swooped silently toward them, but Sally's reflexes were so good that she dodged them easily. They couldn't damage Maple at all, so she just ignored them.

They went on like this for an hour and a half.

"Uh, Sally...do you see something shining up ahead?" Maple said, pointing.

Sally squinted in the direction indicated. There *was* a faint glow.

"Might be a player... Approach with caution."

"Got it."

They crept silently closer.

"It's, uh..."

"...Bamboo?"

It was definitely a bamboo thicket.

But part of one trunk was glowing faintly.

"Wh-what do you think? Should we split it open?"

"I just hope there isn't a person inside," Sally joked.

Glowing bamboo meant only one thing to anyone familiar with Japanese folktales. The legend of Princess Kaguya.

"But...it might be a medal. There are supposed to be some medals you can find just exploring, right?"

They talked it over a few minutes longer but ultimately decided it was worth splitting open the bamboo.

Sally swung her dagger.

There was a satisfying *shunk*, and the glow got brighter.

Their fears proved groundless—inside was a single silver medal.

"Nice! No obnoxious side quests, just a medal."

"Now we only need twelve more!"

This conclusion might have been a bit premature.

There was a rustling in the brush around them, and a bunch of horned rabbits popped out.

"Moon rabbits?"

"Maybe…and those horns might be piercing. Careful."

"Roger that!"

They braced for combat.

Maple was acting a lot more like a typical player than she had when she first started out.

Other than her stats, obviously.

These bunnies were definitely cuter than the bird boss.

But they came charging in, so the two girls fought back.

When the dust settled, the bamboo thicket was a lake of poison, and the bulk of the trees had been felled.

Each rabbit on its own had posed little threat, but there had been a *lot* of them.

"T-too many…"

"Well over a hundred…maybe even two… I'm so tired…"

The bunnies had swarmed the thicket like they owned the place, and it had been a serious workout.

"Wanna climb another tree and rest up?"

"Yeah…that sounds good."

This one medal had taken an awful lot out of them.

But the third day was only just getting started.

Up the tree, they took turns sleeping, climbing down only once the sun had risen.

They were quite deep in the woods by this point, so they were both fretting about finding anything else worth exploring.

"Where to, Maple?"

"I say…straight ahead! Let's carve our way out of this forest!"

"Cool. Works for me!"

They kept the ruins behind them once more, aiming for the far side of the woods.

After another half-hour walk, Sally lowered her voice.

"Maple," she said, "there's a group of players waiting for us in the brush to the right."

Sally wasn't relying solely on Presence Detect. She was also using the sounds of the brush moving and the telltale clinking of armor. This gave her advance warning of monster and player alike.

Acting natural, they walked on, conversing under their breath.

"Likely not that strong—they're hoping to catch us with our guards down."

"Should we capture them?"

"Can you?"

"Yup."

Maple slid New Moon an inch out of its sheath.

"Paralyze Shout."

She slammed the blade back into the scabbard, and the scraping sound echoed through the woods.

Groans went up from the brush behind them.

"See?"

"Flawless. You're so good!"

They parted the brush and found two players on the ground, helplessly immobilized.

"Try again some other time. Just be prepared to always have the tables turned on you!"

Sally quickly finished them off.

No medals.

"Only a fool would try and take you on, Maple. I sure wouldn't risk it…"

Since the event started, they'd crossed paths with other players four times.

Two of those encounters had led to combat, but neither opponent had posed much of a threat. Chrome's party had been the only major foe, but they'd handled that one diplomatically. So far, PVP had not proven to be much of a challenge.

"Five more days, including today. Odds are high we'll bump into stronger players eventually."

If the current rate of two encounters a day held steady, they were in for an estimated ten more.

And at least one of those seemed likely to include a player who had hit the upper ranks in the previous event.

They had to be prepared for an attack at any time.

There *were* players out there in their league.

After another hour of forest trekking, more sunlight started filtering through the trees.

At long last, they could see the land beyond.

"Oh…"

"Wow."

A deep canyon spread out before them.

They were on top of the highest cliff for miles around.

Plenty of shrubs clung to the cliff walls, and they could hear birds singing.

The floor of the valley was shrouded in mist, offering no clue what might lay beneath it.

If they wanted to explore this place, the first order of business was to get to the bottom.

"Think anyone's been through it?"

"No way to know for sure, but given the size of it, I bet there's still more to find."

Like Maple said, the canyon was huge.

The drop from the cliff they stood on was over a hundred yards.

And the canyon wasn't exactly narrow.

It was as wide as the cliff was tall.

"I agree. Let me see if I can find a way down."

Sally examined the cliff face for a minute, searching for footholds. Then she began slowly working her way down.

"Hmm...doesn't seem like there's anywhere you could land, Maple."

Cover Move had a limited range. And with Maple's Strength, dangling from the rocky handholds was essentially impossible for her. Nor did she have Sally's Agility, so swiftly clambering down was out of the question. Maple's extreme build left her unable to get down the cliff on her own, so Sally was looking for larger outcrops—without success.

Sally privately suspected that Maple might be able to soak up the fall damage, but there was no guarantee of that. She decided to not suggest jumping.

"Uh, well, if you find anywhere I could land, lemme know. If you don't, just keep climbing all the way to the bottom."

Maple had a blue screen up in front of her. Maybe checking the time.

"Yeah? All righty, then."

Sally started scrambling downward. There was definitely nowhere Maple could land.

It took Sally a good two hours to make her way to the bottom.

"Well, I made it, at least... Guess I'd better let Maple know."

She'd been sending Maple the occasional progress update via the in-game messaging system.

And this time, she reported the successful end to her climb.

Maple's reply arrived less than a minute later. All it said was:

"Stand clear!"

"Wh-what's she planning...?"

Sally sent a confirmation and backed well away, then climbed a nearby tree for a better view.

"Yikes...even for her, that's..."

Sally was looking up at a giant purple ball. A good ten yards in diameter.

As Sally watched...

...it rolled over the edge, bouncing down the side of the cliff.

Every time it came in contact with the ground, anything it touched dissolved—and the ball itself shrank accordingly.

When it finally reached the bottom, the impact sent sticky goo in all directions.

"S-so dizzy...," Maple moaned, staggering out of the remains of the purple sphere.

Sally hopped out of the tree and went over to her...

Well, not too close, since she couldn't risk touching any of that poisonous goo.

"So? What *is* this stuff?"

"Um, it's called Venom Capsule. A skill that traps a target in a ball of poison. They can't get out easily, so…"

So it was pretty durable.

Maple was still too dizzy to finish the thought, but Sally got the gist. This was *clearly* not the intended use of the skill.

"If you don't have Poison Nullification, it'll drain your HP. Be careful if you ever use it, Sally."

"I never will."

Maple finally recovered enough to walk straight, so they headed off down the canyon floor.

The slope was still pretty steep. Every now and then, there were fairly major drops. With the thick mist, they couldn't see that far ahead, making the precarious ledges harder to spot as well.

"I can't see at all…"

"But that means there might be medals that got overlooked. Maple, be on the lookout for ambushes. And sudden drops."

"Got it! Eyes peeled!"

Of course, it would take a serious drop to do any damage to Maple.

Less of a drop than a cliff, really.

But since they could see only a few yards ahead, they had to carefully pick their way forward.

"Mm? Is that water I hear?"

"Oh? You're right! There must be water nearby."

They headed toward the sound.

Some bat monsters attacked them along the way, but…they were kind of a joke.

The monsters around here weren't very high-level.

"Found it!"

There was a small river in front of them.

A short drop created a mini waterfall, and the sounds they'd heard came from the clear water flowing over the edge.

"Look at that!"

Maple pointed at the rock face opposite. There was a crack in the stone, and they could just make out a cave within.

Thinking it might be a dungeon, they moved closer, but it wasn't very deep, and there were no signs of any monsters. It was just a big fissure.

"Let's make this our base. Exploring this canyon could take a while…"

It was nothing but a gap in the rock face, but it was more than enough to make it their base camp. Certainly safer than up a tree somewhere.

"No complaints! Also, we should check on our eggs."

"Oh, right. We've gotta warm them somehow?"

They settled down in their fissure base, taking a break.

And pulled up their status menus to examine the eggs.

CHAPTER 5

Defense Build and Canyon Exploration

"Hokay, still an egg."

Sally had settled down on the floor of the fissure and taken her egg out of her inventory.

"Are these gonna disappear if we leave 'em out?" Maple asked, worried.

Gear, potions, and other items would vanish two hours after being removed from your inventory.

"Good question. Just to be safe, we'd better stick them back in our inventories before the two-hour mark."

They'd fought hard to get these eggs, and it seemed unlikely they'd ever find replacements. Best not risk losing them.

"Good plan."

"But how do we warm them?"

"Uh…body contact?"

Maple shed her armor and shield and cradled the green egg gently in her arms.

"I wonder what'll hatch?"

She clearly couldn't wait. She was stroking the egg's surface, smiling happily.

Sally decided to warm her egg the same way.

"What matters most is love! Love!"

"Uh, sure."

Gently nestling their eggs, they began planning the next round of exploration.

"I say we just follow the river. That'll make it easy to get back here."

With the mist this thick, they needed a clear landmark or they'd soon get lost.

This map had already proven itself ambush prone, so losing sight of their safe resting point could cause them to lose focus, which would in turn increase the chance of an ambush succeeding.

While Maple might have been able to weather just about any attack, Sally would undoubtedly be in real trouble. With a Vitality of zero, any attack was dangerous.

It wasn't all bad news—that constant danger kept her evasive abilities honed.

The thing was…those life-saving evasive abilities also took a lot of concentration.

Concentration that had already been exhausted beyond measure.

"Sounds good! Let's stick to the river."

They warmed the eggs another hour, but there were no signs of them hatching.

They put the eggs back in their inventories and got ready to explore some more.

"All righty! Let's find ourselves some medals!"

"Woo!"

They set out in high spirits, following the river upstream.

According to Sally:

"Places like this often have something hidden at the source."

This made a lot of sense to Maple. If she was designing a game level, she'd definitely hide things at significant landmarks.

A river's starting and ending points certainly seemed to qualify.

"Can't wait to see what's up there!"

"There's no guarantee anything is, remember?"

"Yeah, I know."

The farther upstream they got, the more jagged the rocks became. Soon it became very hard to walk normally.

"Maple! Use Cover Move to follow me up this bit."

"Got it! Cover Move!"

They repeated this approach any time the terrain got too rough for Maple. Sally nimbly scrambled ahead, and Maple warped over to her.

They kept this up for an hour.

Their camp must have been quite far upstream to begin with, because they reached the source a lot faster than they'd expected.

It was a clear spring, a good three yards across.

A near-perfect circle, the place could be summed up, in their impression, with the word *sacred*.

The mist shrouding it definitely helped sell that vibe.

"It looks...deep," Sally said, peering in.

For such a small spring, it seemed to go a long way down.

"Thinking about diving in?"

"Worth a shot. Not many players have Swimming and Diving skills...so even if they found this place, they might have passed up the opportunity."

"Then go for it!"

"I think I will!"

Sally jumped in the spring and dived under.

Down, down, down, beyond the reach of light.

She swam for ten minutes—and found a decrepit chest at the bottom.

Wary of traps, she carefully lifted the lid.

Inside was a silver wand. There were red and blue gems embedded in the tip.

Sally made extra sure there were no medals here, then swam back to the surface.

"*Gasp!* Whew."

Sally emerged from the spring, dripping.

"Well?"

"Total letdown. Just a wand."

"Oh…shame. What are the stats?"

"Lemme check. Water Magic Up, Fire Magic Up. Wanna see?"

"Sure!"

Sally showed Maple the screen.

Magic Stone Wand

[INT +10] [MP +10] [Water Magic Up] [Fire Magic Up]

"We don't need this, then. Neither of us can even equip it."

"That's true. What now? Wanna go explore somewhere else?"

"Hmm…let's head back to the base, see if we notice anything on the way."

"Good plan. This canyon's so big, it would make sense for there to be at least one other thing!"

They turned around, keeping their eyes peeled.

On the way, they checked both banks, keeping the water in sight, but found nothing.

And eventually they were back at their base.

"Now what? We could just go on downstream, but…that could get tough."

"Yeah. Maybe we should just spend the rest of the day warming our eggs."

With this mist, Sally had to keep her focus at max, and all that swimming had worn her out. She decided to go along with Maple's suggestion.

"Eggy, eggy…oh, there it is."

"Hokay."

They both took out their eggs, cradling and stroking them.

"It's so smooth! This is strangely relaxing," Sally said, leaning back against the rocky wall.

The texture resembled expensive china. Maple thought she could happily caress it forever.

"They don't seem to be hatching, though."

"Well, eggs don't usually hatch overnight."

For three hours, they warmed the eggs, stopping only to put them back in their inventory momentarily.

While they cared for their eggs, they chatted.

"What do you think will hatch?"

"Mine's purple, and yours is green, so…hmm. Maybe you'll get an herbivore? Or something green? Like a snake?"

"Are there green snakes?"

"If it's a monster, why not? I think there probably are real green snakes in, like, tropical areas. But I guess that just proves there's no real way to tell what these will be."

This *was* a video game. Pretty much anything you could imagine might be inside these eggs.

"I hope it's something cute," Maple said.

One animal after another floated into her mind. There were *lots* of cute animals out there. But she could also think of a lot of *not* cute animals.

At the very least, she'd prefer to not get a bug.

"What's mine gonna be?" Sally asked.

Her egg was purple.

Maple tried to think of anything an egg like that might hatch.

"Purple...purple...um...maybe a Hydra?"

"Uh...I think I'd rather not..."

If a Hydra came out and tried to help her in battle, Sally would wind up surrounded by a lake of poison.

And that would make it rather hard for her to move.

"A Hydra...yeah, no. I'd rather something a bit more...docile."

For now, all they could do was imagine the possibilities.

Talking about their hopes and fears, they held the eggs to them, keeping them warm, holding them gently to avoid cracking them.

Deep down, both of them were pretty sure they'd love whatever kind of monster came out.

Maybe those feelings got through.

Cracks appeared on the surface of both eggs.

""Ohhh?!""

"Wh-wh-wh-what do we do?!"

"L-l-let's just...set 'em down?"

They carefully set the eggs on flat, stable bits of ground and lay down next to the eggs, watching closely.

The eggs split open…

And two monsters emerged.

"Wow!"

"They hatched!"

Both girls were delighted.

The green egg had hatched a turtle, slightly smaller than the egg itself.

The turtle's body was the exact same shade of green the egg had been. It was moving slowly around.

The purple egg, meanwhile, had hatched a fox with fur as white as snow.

The fox stretched a few times, like it was getting used to its body. Then purple flames appeared in the air around it, and it stared up at its own magic, fascinated by it.

"Whoa…a fox…from an egg. That I did not see coming."

"I guess ordinary logic doesn't really apply to monsters!"

As they spoke, the turtle moved toward Maple and the fox toward Sally.

The two girls gingerly reached out and patted their respective creatures' heads. Both monsters looked happy.

Then the shattered eggs began to glow.

The light grew brighter and changed shape—forming two rings, one purple, one green.

Maple and Sally reached out to pick theirs up.

*   *   *

"Let's see, the name is…Bonding Bridge? Equipping this… makes it possible to fight alongside specific monsters! Wow. I guess we've gotta put these on."

Sally had explained only the ring's primary function. Maple read the rest with her own two eyes.

Bonding Bridge

While equipped, certain monsters will fight alongside user.
Each ring enables use of a specific monster.
If the monster dies, it will sleep inside the ring and will be unavailable for a full day.

That was a lot better than vanishing permanently.

Permadeath would mean they'd have to be very careful about what fights they brought the monsters to.

"Hmm…a ring, though… My accessory slots are already full. I guess I'd better take off the Forest Queen Bee Ring. I can always use Meditation to recover my HP."

They put on the rings, and the two monsters wriggled with glee.

"Ah-ha-ha, that tickles!"

"Mm! So fluffy!"

They played for a few minutes, but then Sally noticed something important.

"Oh, we can see their stats now."

Perhaps a side benefit to the rings—there was now a second stat screen below their own.

The girls took a closer look.

No Name

Lv1   HP 250/250   MP 30/30

[STR 30]   [VIT 150]
[AGI 15]   [DEX 10]
[INT 20]

Skills

Snap

No Name

Lv1   HP 80/80   MP 120/120

[STR 10]   [VIT 15]
[AGI 70]   [DEX 75]
[INT 90]

Skills

Fox Fire

The first was the turtle, the second the fox.

It seemed like monsters found in eggs started out with some pretty good stats.

"'No Name'…well, we've gotta fix that!"

"Yeah, good point."

They considered this carefully.

And while they pondered the matter, the two monsters played with each other.

It seemed they had become fast friends.

"Okay, I've made up my mind!"

"Yup. Me too."

Decisions made, they approached their monsters.

And made eye contact.

"Turtle, your name is Syrup! Together, we are Maple Syrup!"

Maple seemed absurdly proud of this.

The turtle seemed to like its name. It rubbed up against her.

Best friends already.

"So…what about Oboro? That work for you?"

Sally seemed to want the fox's input. It bounded up to her shoulder and wound itself around her neck. She interpreted this as approval.

Now she had a fox for a scarf.

There was a moment of bliss…

And then Maple let out a shriek.

She was staring at the screen in front of her.

"W-wait, does this mean…?!"

"Mm? What's up?"

Sally came over to look.

"Eep? Ah! D-don't—"

"Oh, I get it."

Sally had seen Maple's screen for all of five seconds, but that was enough.

Maple had been staring at Syrup's stats—and at one stat in

particular. And Sally's observation skills were high enough to know exactly what it was Maple didn't want her to see.

"Maple...you've got less Agility than a turtle."

"Hrngg!!"

Syrup had an AGI of 15. And Maple...was still at 0.

"*The Tortoise and the Maple...*"

"I'm not a folktale! If we raced, I'd win! My legs are longer!"

"Sure. Prove it."

"Er...I-I'd rather not... Ah-ha, ah-ha-ha-ha..."

If she actually lost, she might never recover.

And then she might be tempted to abandon her build concept and actually put some points in Agility.

This was a very real fear.

So Maple decided not to risk it.

Perhaps this was the coward's way out.

"Do the stats mirror whoever warmed the egg? You and Syrup are both heavy on the defense, while Oboro is super nimble."

"Makes sense."

They looked back at the stat screens.

"We can't put any equipment on them, but...it seems like they can level up, right?"

"I wonder if they get stat points when they do? Or do the stats just automatically increase?"

Details like that had not been included in the ring description.

"Guess we should go get them some levels and find out!"

"Yeah...but I don't want to risk them dying..." Sally's fox had moved from her neck to the top of her head. She reached up and stroked its fur.

"Should I capture some monsters, then?"

"That…might be a really good idea. Let's get them a few levels that way."

Maple rubbed Syrup's head, told it to wait there, and then went outside to round up some helpless foes.

Ten minutes later…
Maple came back with a bat in each hand.
They were paralyzed and unable to resist.
Maple dropped them on the ground.

"Um…Syrup! Snap!"
"Oboro! Fox Fire!"
Syrup bit a bat.
Oboro burned one with purple fire.
Both bats let out a spray of red sparks, turned to light, and vanished.

"Aw…it didn't level up."
"Neither did mine."
"I feel like…they're both children of pretty strong species. So they probably need a *lot* of XP."

One of these bats would definitely be enough to get a starting player a level, so that seemed a likely explanation.

"Do we need more, then?"
"If you don't mind? I don't have any skills that'll be much help…"
"Fair! The right girl for the right job! Just watch out for Syrup while I'm gone."
"Fear not! I'll guard it with my life!"
Laughing at Sally's answer, Maple went back out.
She returned twenty minutes later.
This time she was carrying eight bats.

*   *   *

"I feel like a mother bird."

"You're basically doing the same thing!"

Bats fell to the floor.

Syrup and Oboro each took out four and gained a level at last.

Syrup

Lv2   HP 300/300   MP 30/30

[STR 35]   [VIT 180]
[AGI 15]   [DEX 10]
[INT 20]

Skills

Snap, Shell Shield

Oboro

Lv2   HP 85/85   MP 130/130

[STR 15]   [VIT 15]
[AGI 85]   [DEX 80]
[INT 95]

Skills

Fox Fire, Flame Pillar

"Looks like the stats take care of themselves."

"Definitely. They shot up a bunch, that's for sure."

These two had promising futures, so Maple went hunting a few more times.

But there weren't many monsters around, and their new friends didn't gain any further levels.

CHAPTER 6

Defense Build and Downstream Exploration

They'd spent the bulk of their third day hatching the eggs and playing with their new monster pals.

It was now past ten. A little late to go out exploring again.

"Uh…what do you think? Should we…?"

"Let's call it a day."

"That's what I was thinking, yeah."

Petting their new partners, they started making plans for the next day.

"Tomorrow we should explore farther downstream and climb the opposite side of the canyon."

"Yeah… Wait, climb?!"

"Yup, same way we came down— Oh."

Maple had not considered this possibility.

How would she escape the canyon depths?

"A-a-a-am I in trouble?"

"…………Good question."

Maple looked to Sally for answers, but Sally didn't have any.

*   *   *

"So, uh, let's explore downstream while looking for a way up. I bet there's *something*."

Given the seemingly insurmountable nature of the problem, it was likely their exploration might last a lot longer than anticipated.

"We'd better head out early, then."

"I'd like to get away from this place before the fourth day ends, yeah."

They decided to start moving at four AM. Until then, they'd take turns sleeping.

"Morning."

"Mornin'!"

With that vital conversation out of the way, they started exploring.

This was the fourth day of the event—meaning they had officially reached the latter half.

More players would have medals now.

Fights for ownership were likely happening everywhere.

And the girls were certainly targets.

They had to be ready to fight at any time.

"See anything?"

"Not yet."

Sally had been scanning their surroundings but had yet to find a dungeon entrance or the glimmer of a magic circle.

They continued farther downstream for two and a half hours.

There were several fights along the way, and both Syrup and Oboro went up another level. This earned them some interesting skills.

Rest was a skill that put them to sleep inside their rings, allowing them to recover HP in safety.

Awaken was the opposite and called them out from inside the rings.

Currently, both were in their rings, napping.

Mostly because the mist was getting thicker, and the girls were anxious that they might lose track of them.

After another half hour of walking...

They reached the end of the river.

The closer they got, the more suspicious they'd become; actually reaching the end turned those suspicions to convictions.

"This has to be the source of the mist."

"For sure."

The mist had gotten so thick, Maple was having trouble seeing Sally—even though they were standing right next to each other.

They stepped closer to the water's edge...

Then a sudden gust of wind blew away the mist, revealing what lay beneath.

Like the river's source, it was a spring—with a pot at the center.

Mist was pouring endlessly from the pot. It looked like the pot was pulling water from the spring and converting it to mist.

"Should we...look closer?"

"............I think we *have* to."

But the second they stepped into the spring...

...the wind died, and thick mist shrouded everything once more.

"Sally, you still there?"

But no answer came.

Maple raised her alert level.

"Agh! Tch...ah!"

Sally's voice. Metal clashing against metal. Sally sounded rattled, which made Maple anxious.

She headed toward the sounds, only to find a pitch-black pit in front of her.

She peered inside but couldn't make out a thing.

This was definitely where Sally's voice was coming from.

"That settles it! I'm going in!"

She shut her eyes and jumped into the pit.

When she opened her eyes again, she saw Sally—spraying red sparks everywhere.

And...

A knight in silver armor, with a gleaming white greatsword.

"Sally!" Maple gasped.

This was the first time she'd ever seen Sally take damage.

Sally saw Maple and jumped back, moving closer to her.

"A-are you okay?!"

"Yeah, mostly..."

Sally was soon wreathed in Heal's glow.

The painful red sparks vanished.

"Stay behind me! I'll stop anything it throws at us!" Maple cried.

She drew New Moon. A purple magic circle emerged from the blade.

The knight raised its sword.

"Hydra!"

A three-headed dragon rushed the knight's position.

The knight swung its sword, going for the Hydra's heads.

But it managed to intercept only one of them.

The other two hit the knight head-on.

The knight groaned and fell to its knees.

Using its sword to support itself, it tried to stand up…

But failed.

Its melting armor began to glow.

The knight lost hope, and the sword slipped from its grasp.

Motes of light drifted skyward, shining even brighter than the knight's armor.

"Much easier than the bird boss!"

She'd been pretty surprised it could cut off a Hydra head, but it had clearly been lacking in defense and health.

At the same time, that only proved even further how insane that bird had been.

"That's that!"

"Heh-heh-heh, check if it dropped a medal."

As always, any drops would be inside a lake of poison.

Which meant it was Maple's job to collect them.

"I hope there's at least one!" she said, taking a step forward.

"Defense Break!"

A sudden cry.

Pain spread across her back.

Maple turned to look and saw blue daggers slashing at her over and over again.

As she reeled, her health was being sapped away by an armor-piercing skill built around rapidly landing hits. Between the speed of the attacks and Maple's own lack of skill with her shield, she never stood a chance of blocking them all.

"Huh? Huh?"

"Ah-ha! Ah-ha-ha! Ah-ha-ha-ha-ha-ha-ha-ha!"

Sally let out a sinister laugh.

"Wh-why?!"

Maple realized her HP bar was actually going down.

She might be in real trouble here.

"Paralyze Shout!"

This attack caused a powerful status ailment.

That was when Maple figured it out.

What stood before her looked like Sally…

…but definitely *wasn't* her.

She was absolutely sure because it was *impossible* to directly damage a party member.

"Ah-ha! Ah-ha-ha-ha!"

"It didn't work?!"

Further evidence this wasn't Sally: She had far too much paralysis resistance.

But she was a match for Sally's speed—no, she was even faster.

"She's been buffed?!"

The doppelgänger let out another sinister cackle before vanishing—then a new burst of red sparks flew from Maple's side.

"Ugh…I can't even keep track of her!"

Her Hydra and great shield did no good if she couldn't even land a blow.

At least this foe's DPS wasn't very high.

But Maple would have to think of something before all her HP was whittled away.

While Maple was fighting a fake Sally…

…Sally was facing off against a fake Maple.

*   *   *

"Yikes…her defense is as broken as the real thing!"

Sally could slash at her in passing, but this had no discernible effect on her health.

Defense this high was a *nightmare*.

"She was always top of my list of people I never wanted to fight, but…"

"Ah-ha-ha-ha! Hydra!"

This Maple-shaped *thing* was using Hydra, too. Sally dodged.

Hydra wasn't exactly fast—it was easy enough to avoid.

But that didn't make the battle any easier to win.

"This…is gonna be exhausting."

Maple and Sally had good reasons to trust each other…

But with the tables turned, they were in deep trouble.

The knight had just been an appetizer.

This was the real fight. They had to find a way to overcome the powers of the one they trusted most.

◆□◆□◆□◆□◆

"Hydra!"

The poison dragon emerged from New Moon.

But it wasn't aimed at the fake Sally.

Maple's blade was pointed at the ground. The dragon splattered against it, spraying poison all around her.

If the real Sally took a single step inside, she'd die instantly.

And if this one intended to cross the poison lake to reach Maple, she'd be forced to leave herself exposed.

Sally had leaped back to avoid the Hydra attack. She came running back in…

Maple watched her closely.

She could tell…

The fake was definitely avoiding all the poison.

"So you *don't* have Poison Nullification!"

Fake Sally used Leap to close the distance, but this gave Maple time to slam her shield home.

She timed it right—but hit nothing.

"Mirage?!"

"Defense Break!"

The fake's true body slashed Maple's exposed side, then used Leap to kick off her body, vaulting back outside the ring of poison.

"Venom Cutter!"

Fake Sally easily dodged this attack—but something about the *way* she dodged struck Maple as odd.

"Oh…so you *aren't* an exact copy."

Fake Sally was faster than real Sally.

They were both good at dodging.

But for the fake, that came purely down to speed.

The real Sally could dodge by a hairbreadth and unleash a counter right after—her fake couldn't.

The real Sally could evade every attack while moving in closer.

The fake Sally was simply using her superior speed to dodge and had no way to turn those defensive maneuvers into offense.

"But if I still can't actually hit her…Meditation!"

Even as Maple grumbled, the ground around her started buckling.

Pillars of earth rose up, blocking her line of sight…

…and giving the fake Sally some valuable footholds.

"Ugh, she's also better at magic?"

"Defense Break!"

Maple swung her shield toward the voice.

She didn't care if it was just Mirage.

She still had plenty of HP.

Once again, her target turned out to be an illusion. More cuts crisscrossed Maple's back.

She kept swinging, but her shield hit only air.

"Clearly I'm in this for the long haul."

A magic circle appeared on New Moon.

Fake Sally saw it and started backing away.

At that distance, nothing Maple did would hit.

"Fine! You want an endurance test, you got one," Maple muttered. "Venom Capsule!"

A two-yard-wide purple sphere appeared. Maple sank into the center of it.

"Meditation!"

She began healing all the damage she'd taken.

And the fake Sally's weapons...were daggers.

If she tried to slice through the sphere to get at Maple inside, she'd wind up coated in poisonous goo.

Plus, it sat at the center of a poison lake to begin with.

Maple was surrounded by a danger zone.

A hellscape where one false move would leave you poisoned.

Fake Sally *might* have Poison Resist, but she definitely didn't have Poison Nullification.

She couldn't negate all the poison damage Hydra did.

"Cyclone Cutter!"

What she *did* have was Wind Magic that outranked what the real Sally could call upon.

A whirlwind surrounded Maple, whittling away at her poisonous walls.

But Hydra was a much higher-tier skill than Wind Magic.

The surface of the sphere rippled, and some of it was torn away—but nothing reached Maple herself.

"Venom Capsule!"

The sphere expanded. Now it was four yards wide.

And so were her poison walls.

Fake Sally was built for swift strikes that continuously stacked small amounts of damage—there was no way she'd ever get past these defenses.

"I'm just gonna wait here until Little Miss Fake runs out of MP."

Without MP, the fake wouldn't be able to hit nearly as often.

That would be an even bigger problem than getting through the poison walls.

Venom Capsule cost 20 MP per use.

And there was nothing Maple could convert to MP with Devour.

In other words, Maple herself was out of MP.

Since Hydra was in a Skill Slot, she got five activations at 0 MP cost every day—but she'd already used those. Her only option was to wait for her automatic MP recovery to kick in.

Fake Sally sent spells relentlessly against the poisonous walls.

This went on for a while.

"Venom Capsule!"

The growth of Maple's merciless wall forced the fake to retreat.

The capsule was now six yards in diameter.

Maple had only one goal in mind.

"If I can't hit her with my attacks…I just have to fill the entire room with this poison capsule! That's my only way to win!"

The epitome of an endurance test.

Maple's path to victory required she back the fake into a corner.

The fake's speed would no longer matter if she had nowhere to run.

Meanwhile, Sally was at a loss.

Nothing could get past Maple's defenses.

And her offensive capabilities could spell death for Sally with even the slightest misstep.

"My only saving grace is that she's way dumber than the real Maple."

Fake Maple just kept spamming Hydra.

And unlike the real Maple, she used her great shield even for minor attacks.

That meant the fake Maple had long since run out of Devour.

But that Hydra spam was also a problem.

Fake Maple had a skill the real one didn't.

Activating that spell meant all the poison Hydra left behind gathered at Maple's side and immediately formed another Hydra.

This effectively allowed her to chain cast Hydra with very little cooldown.

Sally had assumed her best path to victory was to make Maple run out of stock on all her limited skills, so the fact that she had an endless supply of Hydra had been a shocking realization.

"Better than her using Paralyze Shout, at least."

Dodging another three-headed dragon, Sally racked her brain, trying to think of a viable plan.

"Ugh...come on...there must be a way..."

Avoiding Hydra was easy enough, so she had time to think.

Sally had tried using Defense Break, but Maple's skills—likely Meditation—had healed her right up.

"You just *had* to keep *that* skill..."

Another Hydra was coming her way.

Sally bounded aside, idly wondering what the real Maple was up to.

"Is she fighting a fake me? Has she already won?"

She was convinced Maple would find a path to victory.

Just as Sally herself had no effective means of fighting a fake Maple, a fake Sally would definitely stand no chance against the real Maple.

Maple's abilities had saved Sally any number of times, so she spoke from experience.

"Fine...trial and error it is. You never know! I might find a way outta this!"

Her mind made up, Sally ran through her skill list, forming a number of plans.

It was clear she couldn't win in her current state.

But what if that changed?

What if she acquired a new skill?

Since Sally wasn't doing any damage to the fake Maple, her foe's attack patterns remained consistent.

She just kept spamming Hydra. That made it easy.

Fake Maple wouldn't change.

Sally had the potential to change.

She figured her best bet was to go all in on that possibility.

"I don't wanna lose to a fake! And I know just what skill to start with."

A glowing effect appeared around her, and she threw herself at the fake Maple.

This would also prove to be an endurance test.

Four hours had passed since their battles began. It was now noon on the fourth day of the event.

Maple's plan had succeeded, and Venom Capsule had finally grown so big, it reached the ceiling.

The room itself was fairly large, but only a quarter of that space was still free of venom.

"Venom Capsule!"

Maple bumped the size up again.

"Whew...almost there!"

Fake Sally was still completely unharmed.

But that didn't matter.

Once the capsule filled the room, no amount of recovery would save her.

Maple's biggest problem had been landing an attack...

But that wasn't a problem any longer.

Fake Sally had no means of escaping her fate.

Another hour later...

"Venom Capsule!"

And the long battle ended at last.

Fake Sally was swallowed up, sprayed damage effects like there was no tomorrow—and vanished.

Maple kept her capsule up a minute after, just in case she had to guard against Mirage, but there was nowhere left for the fake to hide.

A medal had also dropped to the floor when she vanished—proof of Maple's victory.

Maple dismissed the capsule.

A rain of poison fell all around her.

"Whew...that was exhausting."

Overcome with a very different kind of fatigue than the bird boss had provided, Maple sank to the ground.

"At least I was inside! I dunno if I could have won outdoors."

Her strategy would not have worked in a zone without finite boundaries.

"Better pick up that medal and take the magic circle outta here. Wonder how Sally's doing? Is she fighting a fake me?"

Maple picked up the medal.

"Will she win? I'm sure she can dodge any attacks, but…"

Growing concerned, she hurried over to the exit circle.

When the light faded, there was a spiral staircase before her.

Light was pouring down from above.

Maple figured it led somewhere important.

"Sally…wouldn't have gone ahead."

Maple decided to wait.

If either of them died, they'd promised to message each other the bad news.

But Maple never saw any such message, so she was sure Sally hadn't been sent back to their starting location.

Either Sally was still fighting and would catch up with her, or they were permanently split up.

And the latter possibility meant Sally wasn't fighting a fake.

It was possible she'd been left behind in the mist, and only Maple had been forced into combat.

But Maple's instincts told her Sally was in a fight of her own.

"If Sally's still fighting… I know! Syrup! Awaken!"

Syrup emerged from her ring.

"Let's cheer Sally on while we wait!"

Syrup and Maple did just that, waiting another hour.

Then a blinding light filled the room.

Just in case, Maple readied her shield, peering over the brim.

"Whew...I actually won..."

The light faded, and Sally emerged.

"...You're...the real one, right?" Maple asked.

Sally looked up, saw Maple, and braced herself, too.

"...We'll need to prove it."

"Fine with me."

Sally's evident suspicion told Maple she'd been fighting a fake, too.

In which case, proof was necessary.

"Are you the Maple I saw bawling her eyes out after getting a shot in sixth grade?!"

"Wh...wh-wh-wh-why did you have to remember that?! Forget it right now!"

This was the last test of identity Maple had expected.

But it was definitely something only Sally would know.

She could see the logic but was so overcome with shame, she ended up involuntarily hiding behind her shield.

Sally already knew this was the real Maple but had felt like teasing her a little.

Exhaustion has that effect on some people.

"Heh-heh-heh...I guess you're real! I knew from the start, of course."

"Wait, I need proof from you, too," Maple said with an intense expression.

"Er..." Sally looked worried.

Maple fixed her with a piercing gaze.

"Are you the same Sally who went in a haunted house in junior high, and halfway through you got so scared that you couldn't walk and a staff member had to carry you crying out the emergency exit?"

"D-don't remind me!"

"The same Sally who got so obsessed with a game that you started keeping a notebook filled with made-up ultimate moves?"

"Wait, stop! I'm sorry! I regret everything!"

"Just paying you back."

"...*Sigh*... I walked right into that one..."

But at least they were together again.

"What were you up to? I was fighting a fake Maple."

"I fought a fake Sally. I won...maybe an hour ago?"

Sally had also received a single medal. She handed it to Maple. Their total medal count was now ten.

"How'd you beat the fake Maple?"

Sally opened her mouth to answer, then closed it again.

"If—just an if—a future event is a tournament? I don't want you mopping the floor with me. So I think I'll keep this one secret."

"Works for me! Hmm. Then maybe I'll keep quiet on how I beat the fake Sally! I don't wanna lose, either!"

Sally kept the means secret, but she did show Maple her stat screen.

"Feel free to guess from my skill list!"

"I'll have to take notes!"

Maple examined Sally's stats carefully.

Sally

Lv21   HP 32/32   MP 25/25 <+35>

[STR 30 <+20>]   [VIT 0]
[AGI 85 <+68>]   [DEX 25 <+20>]
[INT 25 <+20>]

Equipment

Head	[Surface Scarf: Mirage]	Body	[Oceanic Coat: Oceanic]
R. Hand	[Deep Sea Dagger]	L. Hand	[Seabed Dagger]
Legs	[Oceanic Clothes]	Feet	[Black Boots]
Accessories	[Bonding Bridge]		
	[None]		
	[None]		

Skills

Slash, Double Slash, Gale Slash, Defense Break
Down Attack, Power Attack, Switch Attack
Fire Ball, Water Ball, Wind Cutter, Cyclone Cutter
Sand Cutter, Dark Ball
Water Wall, Wind Wall, Refresh, Heal
Affliction III
Strength Boost (S), Combo Boost (S), Martial Arts V
MP Boost (S), MP Cost Down (S), MP Recovery Speed
Boost (S), Poison Resist (S)
Gathering Speed Boost (S)
Dagger Mastery II, Magic Mastery II

Fire Magic I, Water Magic II, Wind Magic III
Earth Magic I, Dark Magic I, Light Magic II
Combo Blade I, Presence Block II, Presence Detect II,
Sneaky Steps I, Leap III
Fishing, Swimming X, Diving X, Cooking I, Jack of All
Trades, Superspeed

"That's a lot of changes."

"Which'll come in handy for the rest of the event."

"I take my eyes off you for a minute and you come back all buffed up!"

"But from this point on, we'll be fighting together."

Sally grinned happily.

Maple smiled back.

"Then let's head up these stairs!"

"Yup. I want more medals!"

The girls climbed the spiral staircase toward the light above.

They emerged at the top of the far canyon wall.

Their long battles had left both girls tired, but they were also running low on time and couldn't afford to kick back.

It was already afternoon on the fourth day.

And medals were first come, first served.

"We've gotta explore *another* forest?" Maple said, looking ahead. It was hard to tell just how deep these woods were. There might be a dungeon within.

"Let's get our heads back in the game! C'mon!"

"All right!"

They stepped into the trees, searching for new dungeons.

Defense Build and Admins 2

Ever since Maple and Sally had defeated Silver Wings, the admins had been regularly checking in on them.

"Maple and Sally cleared the doppelgängers!"

"Ah…yeah, those wouldn't be enough to stop *them*."

"Really? I mean, I intended them to be pretty dang tough!" said the man who'd designed that boss fight.

He'd at least been confident the outcome wasn't a foregone conclusion.

"Lemme check on the others… I put doppelgängers all over the map, so… Oh, here are the fight records!"

He tapped a few keys and put the image up on the big screen.

A player with a spear was fighting a greatsword-wielding doppelgänger.

"Equipment and level…mid-tier."

"So about right for this difficulty level."

One eye on their own work, the admins watched the battle play out.

* * *

The longer the fight went, the more tired the player got—and the more the tides turned against him.

The doppelgänger's attacks started slipping past his defenses, and ultimately a powerful blow cleaved the player in two, and he vanished in a burst of light.

"That's what I'm talking about! The copies should be several steps stronger than the actual players! If Maple and Sally beat them easily, that's because they're *good*."

"Both fights lasted ages... Maple was one thing, but Sally should have worn herself out long before it ended. I mean, she never stops moving..."

"If you want to tire Maple out, you've gotta make her move. She's ridiculous even if she's just standing still!"

"And those tamed monsters are gonna keep getting stronger... What do we do?"

"Uh...I'm working on it..."

The other player's death had reminded everyone what "normal" looked like and drove home how OP the girls really were.

"Keep us posted on anything weird that happens...and anything Maple-related."

"Will do."

And that meant the admins were forced to keep permanent tabs on them.

CHAPTER 7

Defense Build and Desert Exploration

The forest had proved much smaller than the earlier ones.

"Oh? We're already out!"

"Wow...a desert!"

A vast expanse of sand stretched before them.

The uniform terrain was broken up only by the occasional cactus.

No signs of any other players.

"Shall we?"

"Totally."

They stepped onto the sand.

"At least we don't get thirsty!"

"Yeah, that would make exploration impossible."

This game didn't simulate dehydration.

And the desert temperatures didn't affect them negatively at all.

The sand pulled at their feet, so exploring here was definitely hard work, but they were making steady progress over the dunes.

*　　*　　*

"There's *nothing* here!"

"Not that I can see."

The dunes themselves were towering. They climbed on, hoping there would be something across the next one.

"Just gotta keep moving forward."

"Yeah…"

They were keeping Oboro and Syrup in their rings.

Maple had tried taking Syrup out once, but the dunes had proven too steep.

The moment the sand shifted, it sent the small turtle rolling back downhill.

And after noticing how much sand got stuck in Oboro's fur, Sally quickly put it away.

She felt sorry for the poor fox.

They crossed dozens of dunes…and at last, they spied an oasis in the distance.

"Finally!"

"Let's make a run for it!"

Surrounded by sand, that patch of green positively sparkled.

They picked up their pace and headed toward it.

"Well? Any signs of a dungeon?"

"Let's split up and check every inch of the place. It's not that big, so it shouldn't take long."

But their thorough investigation just proved there was nothing here at all.

"Hmm… This is a whole lotta nothing."

"That's disappointing."

"I guess we could rest a bit."

"Good idea. Today is definitely catching up with me," Sally said, stretching.

Both of them had already spent several hours in combat.

And that did take its toll.

Maple flopped down on the ground, looking around her.

"Hmm...uh. Sally! Someone's coming!"

She scrambled back to her feet, raising her shield.

Sally drew her daggers, eyes locked on the approaching player.

"Already occupied...and it's *Maple*. I have no luck."

The approaching player was a grown woman dressed in traditional Japanese clothing.

She wore a kimono the color of cherry blossoms and purple *hakama*.

And with a katana at her side, she was instantly recognizable.

"She came in sixth in the last event."

"What? Really?!"

"I looked into it. I know the top players."

"I hate to interrupt," the woman said. "But is peace an option?"

It seemed like she wasn't looking for a fight.

She said as much...but that might not be her actual intent.

".........Do you *mean* that?" Sally said, watching her closely.

"I could certainly use more medals. If you'd rather fight...then I'll at least try to take one of you down with me."

When she said "one of you," her eyes clearly turned toward Sally.

Maple's hackles went up a notch. She was ready to attack or defend, as needed.

"But in that case, the survivor would get all the medals. That gives us quite an advantage," Sally muttered.

Kimono Lady wasn't the only one looking for medals.

"………True."

"Game on?"

"Up to you, Sally. I don't really… I mean, if we have to, I'll do my part."

Their eyes locked on the woman—

"Superspeed!"

—who immediately turned and ran.

Too fast for the eye to see.

"Superspeed!" Sally ran after her.

Also too fast for the eye to see.

Sally had decided this opportunity was too good to pass up.

"Wait for meeee!" Maple yelled, doing her best to follow.

But this was like a turtle chasing after a hare.

Who wouldn't want to chase someone who ran? Sally went with the flow, ready for combat.

"Wh-why do you know Superspeed?!"

"Why *wouldn't* I?"

Both of them ran out into a valley between two dunes. There was no escape.

The woman turned and drew her katana.

She'd definitely assumed she could win as long as she didn't have to face Maple.

After all, she'd come in sixth.

"First Blade: Heat Haze."

The woman shimmered—then vanished from sight.

*   *   *

And reappeared right in front of Sally.

Her blade swung horizontally, cutting Sally in two.

"What...?!" she gasped.

Her target had vanished, melting into thin air.

"Everyone does that the first time."

Red sparks sprayed from the woman's body.

Sally didn't have high attack capabilities, so she didn't do a *lot* of damage, but she'd slashed the woman's side in passing.

She quickly jumped back, keeping her distance.

"Think you can take me before Maple gets here?" Sally grinned.

"Hrngg... First Blade: Heat Haze!"

The woman closed the distance again...

The same horizontal slash.

"I've seen that one already."

What happened next was hard to believe.

Sally ducked under the katana's swing, charging forward.

And as her opponent's blade hit nothing but air, Sally slipped past on her left, scraping the ground.

"Hngg!"

Red sparks flew from the woman's feet.

"I didn't imagine you would be *this* good. But I suppose that's why you're with Maple..."

"Thanks for the compliment."

They faced off once more.

Sally wasn't making the first move.

Her plan was to evade the woman's attacks and take advantage of the openings they left behind.

If any of these attacks hit, Sally would be done.

But her opponent was unaware of that.

*   *   *

"...I can't die here," the kimono lady muttered.

A change swept over her.

Her beautiful black hair turned white as snow, and her eyes took on a scarlet glow.

An aura glimmered in the air around her, the same cherry-blossom pink as her kimono.

"..............."

Sally didn't say a word, heightening her concentration.

This was Sally's trump card.

An ability no one else could match.

"Final Blade: Misty Moon."

A flurry of strikes came at Sally.

So fast, the blade itself blurred and vanished from sight.

So fast, it was impossible for the naked eye to see.

".........!"

The kimono lady gasped.

Her fastest combo...had failed to land a hit.

The cost of a combo skill was that your movements were limited until the combo ended.

All she could do was keep swinging, hoping it would strike home.

And Sally dodged it all.

The movements of her opponent's feet.

The direction of her gaze.

The shifting of her arms.

The bend of her shoulders.

The sound of the blade.

All these things told her where the next swing would be, and she dodged by a hairbreadth.

Any opponent would find this unnerving. She was evading every swing with the absolute minimum motion.

It was almost like…

The katana was avoiding Sally.

Each swing of the twelve-stroke combo should have been fatal.

When it ended, the woman smiled at Sally and fell over backward.

"I've lost. Make it quick," she said.

Her hair and eyes were back to normal.

The intense aura had vanished as well.

"That was pretty close for me, too," Sally said.

"I'll hit you next time."

Sally raised her daggers high, about to strike…

"Aghhhhhhhhhhhhhh?! I can't stooooooop!"

They turned toward the scream and saw a black mass rolling down the dune toward them, spraying sand in its wake.

"Wha—? Crap! Maple?! No, wait!"

Yes—this black mass was all Maple.

The only silver lining was that she'd unequipped her shield.

But she was clearly past "waiting" or "stopping."

Maple came barreling right toward them.

Plumes of sand rose into the air.

None of them reacted in time.

*　　*　　*

And none of them was prepared for the change happening below.

"Wha—?!"
"Argh, too late!"
"Huh? Huh?!"

These reactions were all they managed before the sand swallowed them up.

Two of them managed to right themselves in the air and land on their feet.

One slammed face-first into the ground with a thunderous *clang*.

Naturally, this was Maple.

Fortunately, it wasn't *that* long a drop, so nobody took damage.

"Wh-what happened?"

"A dungeon with a three-person trigger? It only reacted once Maple arrived..."

Sally scratched her head, trying to figure out their next step. And as she did...

Everyone noticed the black chains linking their arms.

"""Huh?"""

Sally's right arm was connected to the kimono lady.

Sally's left, to Maple.

Maple and the lady had their other hands free.

The chains were about a yard long—which definitely made most ordinary movements inconvenient, if not outright impossible.

*   *   *

It took them all a minute to come to terms with this new development.

"Hngg…they're not coming off."

Sally was rattling the chains, but clearly brute force wasn't gonna be enough.

"There's a button on my wrist!"

"Same here."

"Yeah, mine too… Guess I was too flustered to notice."

After a brief consultation, Sally pressed the button on one of her wrists.

All it did was make a blue screen pop up, like one of their game menus.

Binding Chains

Cursed chains that link three explorers.
Those bound share their fates—the death of one means the death of all.
[Indestructible]

"Whoa, that's…rough."

The predicament affected Sally the most. She didn't have much HP to begin with, and now she'd be unable to dodge effectively.

They tried the other buttons, but they all displayed the same screen.

*   *   *

"I'll defend you with my life!" Maple cried, raising her shield.

"That really is our only option," Sally said, nodding.

Their faith in each other was clear.

"I feel rather out of place now," said the odd woman out.

"...Truce?"

"Seems best. I certainly have no desire to fight."

The kimono lady paused, then introduced herself.

Her name was Kasumi.

Not to state the obvious, but she was a master of katana combat.

This dungeon was going to be rough, and they needed to focus on enemies, not one another—so all tension among the three young women quickly vanished.

"So...should we head out?"

"Sounds good!"

"I agree. Standing around will get us nowhere. And clearing this dungeon may free us from these chains."

Before them was a staircase carved from sandstone. They headed down it.

"Depending on the pattern, the boss could be an issue."

"Let's pray it doesn't have any AOEs."

Kasumi and Sally were both focused on the view below. Maple was happily looking around.

"Humidity's higher here."

"Huh? Oh...you're right."

"Walls are looking cave-like, too. They've gone from smoothly carved to...naturally formed bumps."

At the base of the stairs, the cave opened up.

Rocky stalactites hung from the ceiling. Echoes of dripping water filled the chamber.

The limestone had a sickening complexion to begin with, and the floor and walls were oddly moist, so the view was not exactly pleasant.

The damp floor was slippery enough that exploring this place would be challenging even without the chains.

"See any monsters?"

"Er, no. Maybe there aren't any?"

They listened closely, but all they could hear were the trickling droplets of water.

"Let's keep moving. I dunno where this place ends… It looks like a real maze, too."

There were several exits from this room alone.

All of them had very high ceilings. Like the central chamber, they were easily ten yards high.

"Watch for attacks from above."

"I was just thinking that. Seems like that sort of dungeon."

"I'd better get ready to guard you, then!"

They picked a path and went that way. After a while, they reached another large chamber.

"Still…nothing, huh?"

"Are they just trying to make us nervous? The encounter rate shouldn't be this low. I mean, it's literally zero right now…"

"Maybe because it's a maze, there's only a boss in it? To make up for how much time it'll take to find the boss room?"

Maple's idea sounded very plausible. The others nodded.

"There are a *lot* of side paths here. This'll take a while."

They kept moving.

The paths took them right, left, up, and down, but there was no sign of any boss room.

And they encountered no monsters at all.

"Ugh, another dead end…"

"Sigh. Guess we'll have to turn back…"

"…………Hmm? Wait, hang on…!"

They stopped and looked at Maple.

She was pointing at a small puddle by the wall at the back of the dead end.

There were bubbles forming in it. Small enough to be easily overlooked, but given how identical every passage in this cave was, the tiniest difference was likely significant.

It may have been pure luck that Maple noticed, but fortunately, she had.

They moved closer, peering into the puddle—and found a single medal at the bottom of it.

When Maple picked it up, the bubbling stopped. They must have been there to draw the eye.

"Wow, I completely missed that."

"As did I."

Kasumi insisted that it was finders keepers—making this medal Maple's. They agreed to follow that rule from this point on.

Any items they came across would belong to the person who found them.

"This suggests the cave might not even have a boss."

"It certainly makes that more likely."

"How so?"

"If there was a boss, you'd get the medals for beating it. Like… everywhere else we've been."

"Oh, right. Good point."

If there were medals hidden in puddles, then finding the hiding spots was likely the point of this dungeon.

"Now we've gotta pay close attention to the ground and walls… Ugh, this is exhausting," Sally grumbled.

Kasumi echoed her thoughts. "I'll keep my eyes peeled. I'd like to get *something* out of this."

Once again, they turned back, leaving the dead end behind.

The cave had a *lot* of dead ends, and they all looked the same, so it was easy to get confused. It was hard to tell if they were making any progress.

"I think I prefer straightforward combat-focused dungeons…"

"I sure do!"

"I would rather fight, myself."

As they agreed, they reached another large chamber.

This place was like an ant farm, but they'd yet to find any ants.

"Oh! Something's glowing!"

"Treasure?"

"Maybe."

They headed toward the center of the room.

The ground there glittered like the Milky Way. Nothing like the limestone around it. The sparkling ground seemed to split the chamber in two. Everyone knelt down for a better look.

"It's…pretty, but not any kind of gem. More like gold dust?"

"It resembles that, but it doesn't look harvestable."

Kasumi scraped at it with her katana but got the same hollow clank that came back any time a player struck an indestructible object.

A vein of ore this broad would have been well worth harvesting for crafting materials, but…

No such luck.

"Is this like the bamboo thicket? Where you can harvest it only at specific times of day?"

"It's certainly a possibility."

"Tell me more," Kasumi said.

Maple told her about the glowing bamboo tree.

"There are medals that only appear at night? And here I was, only exploring in daylight."

"What time is it now?"

"Hang on…five thirty. If we find an exit, it'll be after dark."

"Then we'll have to spend the night here."

"Oof, that sounds rough."

But they'd yet to find any signs of an exit, so what choice did they have?

They left the glittering vein behind, exploring further.

All three were watching the floors and walls but had discovered little else since that lone medal.

"Mm?"

"What's up, Sally?"

"Find something?"

"No, just…did you feel the ground shake?"

"I don't think so? Not that I noticed."

"Me neither. Are you sure?"

"Hmm…I might just be tired. I had to fight a fake Maple, after all…"

"A fake Maple? Good lord."

"Yeah, it was a doozy!"

Maple told Kasumi all about the fakes.

Kasumi clearly enjoyed the tale.

"That does sound like a challenging fight. Meanwhile, all I did was explore…"

"Well, tell us about your explorations!"

"Ha-ha-ha, I'd be glad to. Let me see, where should I begin…?"

Being chained together was certainly helping them bond.

Sally had already decided she liked Kasumi too much to take her out.

It was past six now.

The fifth day was almost upon them.

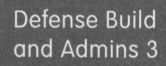

Defense Build and Admins 3

"Maple's on the move! She's fallen into the underground dungeon!"

The admin's cry broke the silence.

Several nearby admins moved to check the screen.

"I thought that place required three?"

"It does. Who'd they add? They'll end up chained together."

If the third player wasn't in Maple's league, they'd be a drag on the other two.

So naturally, all the admins were curious.

"Hold on—bringing it up now."

A few keyboard taps, and Kasumi's data appeared on-screen.

"Oh no! No, no, no! She's not gonna drag anyone down!"

"If anything, Maple's gonna be the deadweight here—the other two have so much more Agility. Just walking around's gonna be an ordeal."

The first man stopped wailing "noooo!" He seemed to be thinking.

"Hmm, it might just do the trick…"

"…Yeah?"

"I agree this dungeon's a good challenge for Maple, but...you think it might?"

"They're all strong players, so they *might* make it through alive...but this matchup could mean we've got a shot at taking one of them down."

From an admin standpoint, dungeons really ought to give players a run for their money.

And for strong players, beating those odds would be all the more exhilarating.

"Well, we can't do anything to interfere. We'll just have to hope for the best."

"Go get 'em, monsters!"

The admins found themselves offering up prayers to their own creations.

CHAPTER 8

Defense Build and Encounters

"Guess we're not getting out of this cave today…"

"Time to start looking for a place to sleep."

With a new goal added to their exploration, they headed on down the passage.

"Sure would be nice to just…stumble across an exit…"

"That would be the best. Today's really taken a lot out of me…"

Maple and Sally were both looking exhausted. They were ready to stop exploring and sleep right here.

Up ahead, they spotted yet another chamber. Then…

"A-an earthquake?!"

"I feel it this time, too!"

The ground was noticeably shaking.

And there was an ominous rumble emanating from the chamber ahead.

All three girls braced themselves for a fight.

It came from one of the other chamber entrances.

Given the height of the ceilings, this thing must be five yards tall and seven yards long.

A giant snail, slowly oozing along.

It didn't seem to notice the girls—it simply crossed the chamber and vanished down another passage.

"..............Crap. That thing is *bad* news."

"I didn't see an HP bar..."

"H-how is that bad?" Maple said, looking very worried.

"If there's no health bar...we can't actually beat it."

"And that means if we want a safe zone, it has to be where that thing can't go...or we're screwed."

The girls were chained together.

None of them could serve as bait.

"Best we move away from here for now. Before it comes back."

"Yeah, let's."

"Uh, how about that passage?"

They picked a third path—neither the one the snail had come from nor the one it had gone down.

"Well, that does explain the dungeon's structure," Sally muttered.

This dungeon was a maze of passages, with many dead ends.

But they all had high ceilings and were free of obstructions.

And the players were chained together.

It was designed to be easy for the snail to traverse and hard for the players to get away.

"Perhaps the difficulty level changes depending on the time of day," Kasumi said.

She was right—the snail only started prowling after six PM.

There was also an end time, but the three of them had no way of knowing it.

And as time passed, the rumbling grew louder.

"I-is there more than one?"

"...........Maybe."

Sally perked up her ears, trying to locate the source of the sound.

She didn't hear any slithering, so she concluded it wasn't that close by.

But they definitely had to stay on high alert.

And that was taking its toll on her already tired senses.

After making it past a few more forks in the tunnels, it finally happened.

"......!"

They rounded a corner...

And found themselves face-to-face with a giant snail.

"Run! Back the way we came!"

Kasumi and Sally started to run, but Maple couldn't keep up.

"Oh...crap!"

Sally tried to get Maple back on her feet, but the snail was already on top of them.

It shook itself, spraying sticky fluid.

"Argh!"

The great shield swallowed the fluid, so by hiding behind Maple, they avoided getting hit.

"Sally, run! Superspeed!"

"! Got it!"

They'd discussed this in advance. Their last resort if there was no other escape.

""Superspeed!""

Both girls turned into blurs.

Maple was dragged along behind them.

Any other player would have sustained fatal damage.
And the party would have been wiped.

But not Maple.
Maple could survive this without taking any damage at all.
Of course, that didn't make it a comfortable ride...
Which was why it was their last resort.

Maple kept bouncing along behind them, her armor clanking loudly.
She'd managed to put her shield away in time, but not her armor.
"How's it looking back there?"
"We're good! It's not keeping up!"
They'd managed to get away this time.
But it would be a while before Superspeed was available again. If they encountered another snail before then, it might well be the end of the road.
And the slithering noise wasn't going away.
"Tch, there's one coming from somewhere else!"
"This way!"
They turned down a side passage.
Maple pulled off her gear, and Sally hoisted her.
A typical approach for them.
"I knew it! The snails are tracking sound!"
Without Maple's armor making a racket, the slithering noises faded away.
"In that case...any nearby?"
"...I think we're good?"
"Whew...we got away..."
They all collapsed against the wall.

They were in the middle of a corridor, not exactly safe—but it was better than a dead end.

"We've…gotta find the exit, or…"
"Yeah…but…"
Their goal was obvious.
The longer they stayed, the worse their odds.
Escaping the dungeon was their top priority.

"This dungeon doesn't seem to have a boss room. If we find medals or equipment, we'll certainly grab them, but…"
"Sounds right. With those snails roaming, it's even more likely the dungeon concept is focused on exploration."
"So, like, the entire dungeon is the boss room?"
"More or less."
Sally got to her feet.
"We'd better move before one finds us. The entrance was from above, so…are we thinking the way out will be below?"
"It might be. No guarantees…"
"Then let's try taking any path that slopes down. Should be better than paths heading up anyway."
The passage they were in was a gentle downward slope. They agreed to follow any paths that did the same.
Down they went.
On the way, they saw several snails in the distance.
And Sally made an important discovery.

The snails were faster than Maple.

If they simply ran for it—they'd never get away.

Any time they turned a corner and came face-to-face with a snail, Sally would have to pick up Maple—delaying the start of their run.

And if they got hit by that sticky projectile, they might wind up trapped.

But if Maple had her shield out to guard against that, Sally couldn't carry her.

They had to avoid getting that close at all costs.

"Whew…gotta stay focused…"

Sally cracked a whip, forcing her tired body into high-focus mode.

Her ability to detect enemies was keeping them alive.

They had to move carefully, without sound…and as they did, the dungeon's very appearance began to change.

"It's pretty…"

"Yeah. It certainly is."

"I think I actually feel less exhausted now?"

There were purple crystals glowing on the walls.

These weren't harvestable, but it did seem like the light was easing their weary minds.

And…

"Is it just me or are the passages getting smaller?"

Sally was right—the ceilings were clearly getting lower, some of them just barely tall enough for the snails to get past.

"But…the tremors are getting bigger."

"So there are more snails, but the terrain is less in their favor?"

They pressed on.

All three of them were hoping they'd find the exit before the day was done.

Praying they wouldn't hear that slithering close by, every sense straining to avoid getting trapped.

◆□◆□◆□◆□◆

"So…do we think there're *any* safe rooms in this place?" Sally whispered.

She was acutely aware that her focus was wavering.

It wouldn't be strange if she made a fatal mistake at any time.

Sally was their best hope of detecting enemies in time, so one mistake would mean all three of them died.

"Gotta keep going," she said, slapping her cheeks. She perked up her ears again. "I hear a faint noise from the path on the left. Right sounds safe."

The other two were listening as well but couldn't make out anything distinct over the constant rumbling.

There was no way either of them could take Sally's place.

"Let's hurry. Before something comes from the right, too."

"Oof, that would be bad."

"Then let's move!"

They hurried down the path to the right.

And encountered no snails on it.

If they'd gone left, they'd have run into a snail.

Sally's detection skills were still functioning—for now.

The path they took led to a dead end.

But this wasn't *entirely* bad news.

*　　*　　*

"I see something!"

Kasumi was pointing at a large purple crystal.

Trapped inside it was an old key and a pair of earrings that looked like cherry blossoms.

They moved closer—and noticed the crystal had an HP bar.

That meant it was destructible.

"That key looks important… I bet we'll need it later."

"That's what I thought, too."

"Allow me."

Kasumi drew her katana.

"Fourth Blade: Whirlwind!"

A slice up and a slice down—twice.

Four quick slashes struck the crystal.

This was more damage than the crystal could sustain, and it shattered with a sound like glass breaking.

The key and earrings fell to the floor, and Kasumi scooped them up, checking them out.

"The key…doesn't have a description. The earrings are just an accessory. They seem unrelated to escaping this place."

She let the others see.

"Mm, looks like it."

"Do we…use this key somewhere?" Maple asked.

"Who knows?" Sally said. She handed the earrings back to Kasumi. "Either way, these are yours."

They discussed things a bit longer and decided Kasumi should hold on to the key as well.

"All right, back the way we came."

This was a dead end, and they could easily get trapped here.

They couldn't afford to linger.

After exploring a while longer, they found a hole near the ceiling.

It was right in the middle of the passage—and not something they'd seen before.

The obvious assumption was that something was hidden inside.

"Can we get to it?"

"Uh…it's too high for Leap…"

It was a good ten yards above them, and Sally couldn't jump that high.

They stopped to think.

"………Wait! Shhh! ……Oh no!"

Sally's ears caught slithering coming their way.

From both directions.

"Argh! I was afraid of a pincer attack!"

They'd managed to avoid it all this time—in fact, their party had avoided having many encounters at all. All because Sally had been so focused on detecting them in time.

Using the direction and size of the tremors to estimate distance and their positions, she'd been carefully picking the best routes.

But their luck had finally run out.

She'd misread one snail's approach.

"That hole's our only way out!"

"Sally, Leap for it! I'll handle the rest!"

There was no time for Kasumi to explain her plan.

Both snails were already in sight.

*   *   *

"Leap!"

Hoping against hope that she could reach it, Sally jumped—but with two others weighing her down, there was no way.

"Third Blade: Blue Moon!"

In midair, Kasumi accelerated.

The system boosted her movement, rocketing her upward.

Dragging the other two along.

Kasumi spun in the air, leaving an attack effect behind and propelling herself forward...

Landing just inside the hole's entrance.

The others were yanked after her, and they all went tumbling through. Sally peered over the edge at the snails below.

They were spitting sticky stuff, but it couldn't reach them up here.

"Looks like they can't follow us!" she said, relieved. She leaned back against the crystal wall, resting.

"Ha-ha...I'm just glad that worked."

"Thanks, Kasumi. Leap alone was nowhere near enough."

"That was amazing!"

"Blue Moon comes with a long recovery time after each use. If that hadn't worked, I'd have been unable to move at all, and the snails would have doomed us. It was a long shot."

But that long shot had paid off.

The three girls could finally get some rest.

This hole wasn't big enough for those snails.

"Rest is good and all, but shouldn't we scope out this hole first? No guarantee there aren't other monsters in here."

".............Good point. You never can tell. I was definitely assuming those snails were the only thing in this dungeon."

"We'd better check, then."

They picked themselves back up and headed deeper in.

It connected to a circular chamber.

It was a five-yard drop to the floor below and had six passages leading in.

Even from a distance, these passages were obviously big enough for snails.

But in the wall opposite the hole—was a door.

Only two yards tall.

Definitely nothing as big as the boss room doors they'd found.

"Think that's the exit?"

"Hang on. Keen Sight! ....There's a keyhole. Likely for the key we found. I think we can assume there's *something* behind it."

"Then…should we? I don't hear any snails coming."

"Oh?"

"You're sure?"

Sally double-checked.

Both passages were silent.

She listened for a full minute but couldn't hear any snails.

"I'm sure. No sounds at all."

"Then…shall we?"

"I'm in!"

They dropped down from the hole.

Maple and Kasumi both trusted Sally's detection skills.

Sally had faith in them, too.

And those skills had given her an accurate answer.

There were no snails approaching. There were no monsters anywhere.

But as events soon proved, they should have taken a rest in that hole.

All three girls were too tired to think straight.

Not one of them realized that dropping down might *change* things.

As they hit the floor, the crystal behind them grew—blocking the hole.

And that awfully familiar sound echoed from every side passage.

That horrible slithering they'd already heard far too much of.

"C-crap!"

"What now?"

"Run for it! That's our only option!"

Maple was in full gear.

But they didn't have time to wait for her to unequip it so they could pick her up. Snails were already crawling out of the passages.

They were twenty-five yards from the door.

Not normally a significant distance, but right now—it seemed very far away.

""Superspeed!""

Sally and Kasumi both blurred, rocketing forward, dragging Maple along behind. Three snails each were coming into the room from the right and the left, two of them on the diagonals ahead.

Those two were spraying sticky stuff everywhere, trying to stop them from reaching the door.

"Hngg…left!"

"Got it!"

Sally and Kasumi quickly veered, following a safe path.

Maple was being dragged after them and couldn't take evasive maneuvers, so she had to use Devour to escape the stickiness.

The snails were faster than Maple, but no match for Sally and Kasumi.

As long as they avoided the sticky goo, reaching the door was simple.

"Kasumi! Key!"

"On it!"

Kasumi popped open her inventory, grabbed the key, and reached for the keyhole.

But then…

"Yikes!"

There was a wet noise, and something shot out of the snail—what could only be called a tentacle.

It snatched the key from her hand.

The tentacle placed the key on the snail's head. Then it withdrew back into the snail's body.

"W-we've gotta get it back!"

"But I can't reach with Leap…!"

Sally alone might be able to manage it, but with Kasumi and Maple in tow, it was too high up.

"Can't stop to think! They're coming!"

The snails were all oozing toward them. Pausing for a second would leave them covered in goo. And they might use those tentacles again.

"Kasumi, would Blue Moon do it?"

"I'd need a safe opening! Or they'll finish me before the recovery period ends!"

More and more of the ground was getting coated in goo.

They didn't have much time left.

It was Maple who broke the impasse.

"……Sally! Run straight toward the hole we came from!" she yelled.

Sally took one glance at her and saw the confidence in her eyes.

"…Got it. Well, here goes nothing!"

Sally and Kasumi raced forward.

Getting back to the hole meant slipping past the snails—

—which already had them surrounded.

"I'll handle that! Sixth Blade: Inferno!"

Her katana ignited, sending scorching flames among the snails.

This did no damage, but it did make them flinch—buying the group enough time to rush past. (They'd tested this on the way here.)

The snails turned to give chase.

"Thought so! They're not too smart," Maple said.

The snails were all following in their footsteps.

This alone told the others what Maple's plan would be.

*　　*　　*

"Hydra!"

"Leap!"

"Third Blade: Blue Moon!"

Each skill did its job.

Maple made the snails flinch, and Kasumi and Sally took that opportunity to vault up to the snails' shells.

Maple's skill had bought enough time that Kasumi could recover from hers.

"No goo up here! And…"

Sally looked ahead. More snails, all following the same behavior.

One of them had the key.

Since the snails had all come after them single file, they formed a line almost all the way to the door.

And by a stroke of luck, the snail with the key had joined the queue last and was parked at an angle.

"We can grab the key without the shell getting in the way!"

"Leap!"

The shell was higher than the snail's head, so all they had to do was hop down and snatch the key back.

"Got it!"

"Hurry!"

But the ground below was in such poor condition, they lost a few precious seconds.

By the time they reached the door again, the snails had had enough time to send sticky goo and tentacles their way.

But…

"Cover!"

Maple's shield blocked them all.

With her on defense, not a single attack could make it through.

"You're not getting us twice!"

"All right! It's open!"

They went tumbling through the door.

The second they were all inside, the doorway vanished—there was no chance of the snails following them now.

And the chain binding them together crumbled away.

They'd successfully cleared the dungeon.

"Whew…we're aliiiive…"

"I'm…so tiiiired…"

"I never wanna see another snail…"

The room had four treasure chests and a magic circle.

"Should we open those up?"

"Ooh, yeah."

They each took one.

"I got a spear!"

"Great shield."

"Mine has a wand."

Amethyst Spear

[STR +20] [VIT +15] [Crystal Wall]

Amethyst Geode

[VIT +30] [Crystal Wall]

> ## Amethyst Wand
> [INT +20] [MP +30] [Crystal Wall]

They each looked them over. The great shield was the only thing any of them could use.

"Maple, you can have this. It does me no good," Kasumi said, handing Maple the Amethyst Geode.
"You're sure?"
"Please take it."
It wasn't exactly a fair trade, but Maple handed the spear over, and Sally added the wand.
"Hmm…they're all good pieces," Kasumi said, checking the stats.
Players who could actually equip these would definitely be interested.

"There's still one chest left."
Sally headed toward it.
The other two peered in as she lifted the lid.

"Hmm…three scrolls. That's it!"
Making doubly sure there weren't any medals, Sally picked up the scrolls.
"They're identical. We can all learn the skill."
She tossed over the spares.
Once everything was back in their inventory, they were done with this place.

*　　*　　*

"Should we go, then?"

"Yeah. Man, that cave was tough. I'm bushed!"

They stepped onto the magic circle and left the dungeon behind.

All three of their unique play styles had helped them make it through intact.

Each had made up for the other two's shortcomings.

At long last, they found themselves in the desert once more.

"Ah...the night sky...!"

"We weren't down there *that* long."

"But it's still a sight for sore eyes."

After several hours in a cave, seeing the sky was an undeniable source of relief.

"So, uh...we meant to fight you, Kasumi. But...I think we're past that."

After all that cooperation, Sally wasn't in the mood to rekindle their battle.

Neither was Maple.

"I'm not looking for a fight, either," Kasumi said. "Not that I ever was..."

"Oh!" Maple said. "Can we add you to our friends list?"

"Mm, certainly."

All three of them registered one another and then flopped down on the sand, gazing up at the sky.

Between the fatigue and the relief, none of them was inclined to do anything else.

"Kasumi, what'll you do next?"

"Hmm. Well, I think we should go our separate ways. Now

that we're friends, we can find each other again once the event's over."

"You could come with us if you want."

"Yeah! Totally!"

"Ha-ha. I appreciate the offer, but not this time. I feel like having two gold medals in the same group would mean we'd be looking at *a lot* more fighting."

That was a very good point.

The other players all knew both Maple and Kasumi had a gold medal each.

That made them tempting targets indeed.

And if they had two—that simply doubled the value of attacking them.

"Oh…it's a shame, but I gotta agree."

"Mm. Okay," Kasumi said, getting to her feet. "I'd better be going."

"Good luck!"

"Same to both of you."

Kasumi waved once and walked off across the sand.

Their unexpected partnership drew to a close.

CHAPTER 9

Defense Build and the Event's Fifth Day

Sometime after Kasumi departed, Sally and Maple rose to their feet.

"We'd better be going, too."

"True."

Their goal was to find a place to sleep.

"Guess we gotta get out of the desert first..."

There was no protection out here, so sleeping in the desert would be very risky.

They started walking.

"It's awfully big..."

"Very."

They crossed dune after dune, but the view never changed.

The dunes themselves were so big, they blocked the view ahead, and the girls weren't even sure if they had their bearings straight.

And the desert wasn't completely devoid of monsters.

Neither of them was in the mood to fight.

"Let's take a rest once we cross this dune."

"Sounds like a plan."

The slope was so steep, they resorted to scrambling up the incline using their hands.

But when they reached the top—they saw something new.

"No more dunes?"

"It's all *flat!*"

It was still a desert but one devoid of elevation shifts.

Not a single dune—if it had been daylight, they could have seen quite a distance.

"Let's head that way?"

"Absolutely. Looks much easier to get around."

They slid down the side of the dune and began walking again.

"If the sun was out, we might have found a landmark to head toward."

"Totally a possibility! How much longer is this event?"

"Three more days. And our goal is another nine medals."

"Hmm…that's feeling pretty tough."

"I think we're gonna need a few PKs."

"Hnggg, right…"

If that was the only option, Maple was willing to consider it, but since there was no telling who had medals or not, it wasn't any easier than hunting for new dungeons.

"Well, we can think about it if we run into any other players. If they wanna fight, we'll just have to beat them."

"Mm, makes sense. If it happens, it happens! And if we can't find enough, that's all there is to it."

Sally had long since discovered it was no use trying to force Maple into anything; instead, she always just proposed whatever seemed most efficient, citing her own experience.

Here, she specifically outlined it as one option, an option they might not even need. Just a card to keep up their sleeve if the situation left them with no choice.

They moved on across the vast desert.

It was too dark to see far ahead, but in the distance, they could hear leaves rustling—and they knew their desert trek was nearly at an end.

"No telling what monsters might be waiting here. Careful!"

"You got it!"

They walked through the darkened forest for a good half hour. And then they found a cave.

"Let's go in. It doesn't look that deep, so it might make a good camp."

"I'll take the lead."

They were worried this might turn out to be another endless cavern, but closer inspection proved it was only five yards deep.

Both girls flopped to the ground, finally able to rest.

"Ugh…that was a *very* long day."

"Seriously."

They each summoned their partner.

Both for the comfort and because they'd been unable to call them out much recently, which made them feel a bit guilty.

"Sorry you had to stay cooped up in there all day."

"Once this event is over, I promise we'll help you grind some levels properly."

They both doled out head pats and back rubs, and their monsters looked thoroughly pleased with the pampering.

"I guess tomorrow we start by exploring this forest. We're definitely done for the day, right?"

"I am for sure."

They went right to bed, sleeping in shifts. After the day they'd had, they needed as much sleep as they could get.

And as they slept, they held Syrup and Oboro in their arms.

◆□◆□◆□◆□◆

Six o'clock the next morning.

They'd banished enough of their fatigue to feel like exploring again.

They had a light breakfast and left the cave to see what this forest had to offer.

Maple had Syrup out and Sally, Oboro. Walking alongside them, Oboro darted this way and that, while Syrup dutifully plodded between them.

"...............」

"Wh-what's that look about, Sally?"

"Syrup is *definitely* faster than you," Sally said, making a big show of comparing the two of them.

Maple quickly picked up Syrup, hugging it close.

Sally's grin just intensified.

They'd explored a *lot* of forests during this event, and this one was particularly unremarkable.

After a solid two hours of searching, they'd found...exactly nothing.

"If there are some special conditions...I can't guess 'em."

"Should we just go on until we come out the other side?" Maple suggested.

Sally considered this proposal a moment, then nodded.

"Which way?" she asked.

"No point turning back, so...straight ahead! Not like we've explored the *entire* forest anyway."

They'd been focused on the forest depths, so if there was anything on the outskirts, they would've missed it.

But the odds of that were not high.

Whether it was a dungeon or a field, anything valuable would normally be hidden in the deepest section, guarded by a powerful foe.

Nobody was just gonna dump a chest with a medal in it right next to the entrance.

And as the girls reached the edge of the forest, they heard a tantalizing sound.

"Are those waves I'm hearing?"

"I think so."

The trees thinned ahead, and beyond that, they saw white sands and a vast swath of ocean. The water was so clear, they could see brightly colored fish darting about at the bottom. The gorgeous coral reefs looked like flowers blooming in the ocean depths.

There was an island in the distance.

Sunlight glinted off the water, and everything sparkled.

"Wow...finally an ocean! This is a *really* big map."

"So much variety!"

Over the last five days, they'd visited a field, several forests, a snowcapped mountain, a canyon, a desert, and a cave.

And now they had an entirely new type of terrain. This felt well worth exploring.

The sheer variety of landscapes they'd found made them all the more eager to see more.

Days and hours spent exploring had brought them to new dungeons and new views.

And so far, they'd been lucky enough to find dungeons no one else had conquered.

"But, uh…I can't explore underwater."

"Then I'll explore for both of us!"

"Okay. Thanks."

Sally dived right on in, took a deep breath, and vanished beneath the waves.

She could stay under for a full forty minutes.

Maple settled in for a long wait.

"What should I do…? Not like I can fish properly. And we've explored the forest already… Hmm, I guess I'll see if there's anything buried on the beach."

Maple began rooting about in the sand.

Meanwhile, Sally was under the sea, enraptured by the jewellike fish flitting around her.

It was a wondrous sight.

After a day spent staring at gross, slimy snails, it seemed all the more beautiful.

But she couldn't spend the whole time gawking. She started poking around among the coral and in the sand on the seafloor.

This would have taken ages without the right skills, but with her build, she could quickly and efficiently check the surrounding area.

"*Gasp*… Found one medal! Maybe not many people have Swimming and Diving. Without those, they can't explore these depths!"

There was no need to push her limits, so she was surfacing for air regularly.

Some of the gaps in the coral went down pretty far, and she'd found the medal in one.

Leading off that, Sally was focusing her efforts on similar locations.

It seemed likely that was the most reliable way to find medals or equipment.

Figuring anything shallow would have been picked clean by now, she was sticking to the deepest areas.

And that rewarded her with a second medal.

"Whew…that just leaves…the island over there, huh?"

She started swimming that way.

The island was much too far out to sea for Maple to reach. It proved quite small, nothing but palm trees—and a staircase in the center.

"Worth a shot!"

Sally picked her way down the stairs.

After approximately one hundred of them, she reached an ordinary wooden door.

Didn't seem to be sealed, didn't have a keyhole, and no magic circles anywhere.

She carefully opened it.

And was quite surprised by the view beyond.

It was a beautiful domed chamber.

And in the center of it was a familiar-looking shrine, with a magic circle next to it.

"Yikes…another one of these…," Sally muttered, inspecting them both.

The previous one had led to the bird boss. Honestly, she didn't really feel up to fighting anything else that high-level.

*   *   *

"Best to head back and see what Maple thinks before anything else."

Sally went up the stairs to the surface.

She'd been too busy diving and exploring to look over her shoulder. Only now did she catch a glimpse of what was going down on the beach.

"Maple...what *are* you doing?"

Even from this distance, she could make it out.

There was a sandcastle on the beach. One clearly taller than Sally herself.

"I guess...I should head on over..."

There was a splash as Sally hit the water. She swam back as fast as she could.

"Wow...it's even bigger up close."

It was *twice* Sally's height.

She heard excited voices coming from within.

She found the entrance, peered around it, and found Maple sitting with a boy.

He had curly red hair and spade-shaped earrings. Pale skin and eyes the same color as his hair. He was only a bit taller than Maple, with androgynous features and a slim, delicate build.

With the exception of those earrings, everything Sally saw looked like default equipment.

Didn't seem like he was carrying any noteworthy weapons, either.

No shields, swords, or wands.

Completely empty-handed.

Sally had never seen this boy before—and here he was, playing Othello with Maple.

"Auuugh, it didn't work!"

"Perfect victory."

The entire board was white.

Maple had obviously picked the color of her signature equipment—black.

Which meant she'd lost. Badly.

Mid-anguished wail, she noticed Sally and hopped to her feet.

"You're back, Sally!"

"Uh, yeah. I am. So…who's your friend?"

"I'm Kanade. Maple and I built this castle together." Kanade turned to Maple. "It was a lot of fun," he said.

"It was!"

Sally was starting to suspect these two had a lot in common.

If their minds were this alike, she could see why they'd made friends instantly.

"Is it safe?"

"I think so? You're safe, right, Kanade?"

"I mean, I'm only level five. Not that it's anything to brag about, but I'm still very weak."

Kanade popped up his stats window and held it up to let Sally see.

He was definitely level 5.

"Y-you showed us that pretty casually."

"Why wouldn't I? You're in Maple's party, right? Then I don't see the problem."

Sally had no clue what had happened while she was gone, but Maple seemed to have earned his complete trust.

And the reverse was also true.

Maple insisted Sally register Kanade as a friend, too.

Maple and Kanade had already friended each other.

"Uh…well, I'm Sally. If Maple says you're cool, then I'll take her word for it. And…"

"And?"

"If you do attack, we can take you easily."

Sally brandished her daggers.

"I—I promise I won't, okay?"

Sally hesitated to say anything with Kanade here, but she told Maple about the dungeon she'd found.

"Ehhh...I don't really wanna..."

"That's what I thought. But we don't actually *know* what's inside, so...it might be worth a look."

"Hmm...I guess..."

There was a long, thoughtful silence...broken by Kanade, of all people.

"Then I can go check it out. My start location is only a hundred yards away."

This proposition was definitely based on the assumption that he would die.

The girls both tried to protest, but he was already on his way.

They watched him swim off into the distance.

"He's got Swimming I, so I guess he'll make it there without issue..."

"Y-you think he'll be fine?"

"I really don't know..."

They watched until he reached the island, wondering what might be inside the whole while.

"What are you thinking?"

"I'm just assuming it's another super-boss."

"Like the bird?"

"Exactly."

But that was just a guess. There was always a chance the circle led to a room filled to the brim with treasure.

"If there's treasure, Kanade might just take it all."

"Hmm…I don't think he would, but…"

Maple put a hand to her brow, surveying the distant island.

Few people would pass up a chance at treasure.

And there was no telling where the transport circle inside would take him—meaning there was no way to give chase.

"Yup, I died," Kanade said after emerging from the woods behind them.

They didn't even need to ask how bad it had been.

This was *just* like the bird.

"Reporting in, Sir Maple."

"Verily? Speak on!"

Where this bit had come from was a mystery, but Sally had done the same sort of thing before, so she let it pass without comment.

"The circle took me somewhere underwater. And this water seemed to slow my movements. I was helpless against the giant squid in there."

"I see… Welp, I'm out!"

Maple couldn't do anything underwater, and if the water had an effect like Sally's Oceanic, then Sally's evasion skills would be equally useless.

There was no point even trying.

Courage and recklessness were different things.

"Let's leave this one be."

"I thought you'd say that."

"I'm gonna scour the seafloor a bit more; then we should move on."

Sally did some stretches, glancing at the sea.

There were still a few areas left to check.

"Should I help? You can have any medals I find."

This was a no-risk, high-return proposition, but…those were usually too good to be true.

"You mean that, Kanade?"

"This is all I really need," he said, taking out…a Rubik's Cube.

"What's that?"

"This is my spoils from this event. I found a portal leading to the floating island that's circling the forest behind us—actually, you can't see it now that I've cleared it. Anyway, this is the wand I got as a reward."

"That cube is a wand?!"

"Yup. The circle took me to an ancient library…and there was a jigsaw puzzle in one room. When I put it together, this popped out. It took me four whole days!"

The event map they were on was an island surrounded by water, and there were several islands floating in the sky above.

"And one of those had a library on it? I guess those *are* part of the map, then!"

Maple stared up at them.

They were hovering over the main island but were still pretty far away. She counted six floating islands, but there might have been more hiding behind the bird boss mountains. It was hard to be sure.

The Rubik's Cube Kanade had found was glowing faintly, floating above his palm.

"This has a skill attached."

"Wow…some of our gear did, too."

"It's called Akashic Records. It's pretty neat."

"How's it work?"

Kanade was about to answer but thought better of it.

"I'll tell you if we ever end up in the same party," he said, flashing a mischievous grin.

Maple decided there was little use pressing the point.

"Hmm…I don't think that's happening soon," she said.

"Ah. Shame!" Kanade grinned happily.

He didn't seem particularly disappointed.

Kanade wasn't like any players she'd met before. He had a unique vibe that made him a little hard to get a read on.

"I'd like to meet again once the event's over."

"Oh, sure! We can play more Othello."

"Anytime."

"With that settled," Sally said, "I'm gonna go explore."

"I'll come, too. The more the merrier, right?"

Sally and Kanade headed out to sea.

Maple decided to search the beach properly this time.

Their scouring didn't turn up anything else.

They'd checked every inch of the beach and the seafloor but came back empty-handed.

There was clearly nothing more to do here.

It was time for them to say good-bye to Kanade and set out in search of new pastures.

"Good luck!"

"Mm. See you around."

And with that, they went their separate ways.

"He's fun but a little odd."

"Yeah? Maybe I'm just too used to you, Maple."

"H-hey, what's that supposed to mean?"

They decided to follow the coastline for now.

This seemed like the best way to avoid getting lost.

◆□◆□◆□◆□◆

Two hours after they'd parted with Kanade...

The elevation had been rising steadily, and they were now following the edge of a cliff.

Meanwhile, the forest on their left had vanished, and they were entering a ruin of moss-covered stone.

This definitely looked promising.

A cobblestone road ran from the town to a prominence that protruded over the waters below.

On this overhang were several standing stones, placed around a pedestal.

They began to explore the run-down homes and dried-up wells—then they heard voices.

"Maple, hide."

"Right."

From the shadows, they scoped out the situation.

There were three players.

These were better equipped than most players they'd encountered; their gear was solidly in the upper rungs of mid-tier.

Nothing that looked like it came from a unique series but probably all boasting solid stats.

Sally assumed they had the levels to match.

They were already quite close. If either girl made a noise at all, they'd be instantly discovered.

"What do you think?" Maple whispered, leaning in.

A voice *that* quiet seemed safe enough, so Sally answered in kind.

"We can choose whether to fight or not. If we're doing this…I can solo them. Or fight alongside you."

Sally deliberately omitted the option of having Maple go in alone.

The other party was talking about something rather interesting.

"Any clue what that book means?"

"Nah, it's in such bad condition—I can only make out fragments. I know it's got *something* to do with water, but where the Ancient Heart is…"

"C'mon! That book's guaranteed to drop if we die. You've gotta figure it out first!"

"I know!"

They turned back to their camp.

Moving away…

…without spotting the girls.

"Maple, I'd like to take them out. But they'll try to protect this 'book' by scattering in all directions. Which means…"

She leaned closer, whispering the plan.

"……Got it. Think it'll work?"

"Heh-heh-heh. I promise!"

The other players were almost out of sight.

If they waited any longer, they'd lose track of them.

So they put their plan in action.

"Yes! A fifth medal!"

A girl's voice echoed through the ruins.

All three players swung toward it, then quickly ducked into cover.

If this girl had five medals, they definitely wanted those for themselves.

But there was no telling how good she was.

They had to scope her out first.

The girl popped up from the shadows, skipping along, all smiles.

She was wearing a scarf as blue as the ocean and shorts a little darker. Beautiful equipment that definitely drew the eye.

But the rest of her?

It was all clearly starting gear.

Just standard clothes. Nothing special at all.

No hidden buffs.

Even her shoes were the default pair.

"What do you think?"

"Clearly a beginner. She's landed a couple of good pieces... Safe to assume she found them during this event. I looked just like that early on, myself—wearing whatever I found."

"No proof she really has those medals."

But even as they watched, the girl opened her inventory and took something out.

Five medals.

"Heh-heh-heh! Halfway there! I just need five more!"

Was this a habit of hers?

She'd plopped down on a nearby wall and was happily inspecting each medal in turn, putting it back in her inventory when she was done.

"That settles it. We're going in."

"Yeah. Take her down."

They rushed out of the shadows, and the girl looked startled.

She drew her dagger and stood up, backing slowly away.

"Wh-what do you want?"

"Sorry, kid. We're gonna help ourselves to your medals."

"...........!"

She turned to run, but they had her surrounded. There was no escape.

Players approaching from three directions, and this girl clearly had no clue what to do. Her legs were shaking, her eyes darting this way and that.

"Now!"

""""Rah!""""

All three swung their weapons...

The girl swung her dagger, but that wasn't nearly enough. Their weapons struck home...

And they knew the medals were theirs.

Except...

There were no medals.

And the girl herself vanished into thin air.

""""Huh?!""""

Even as they cried out in shock, red sparks erupted from one of them.

A second hit. A third.

The player gaped at the damage—and then took even more.

This proved fatal.

"Sorry. I'm gonna help myself to your book."

The book fell to the ground, and it was scooped up by the girl—the same one they'd all thought was an easy target.

"Huh? G-give it back!"

None of this made sense. One of the survivors snapped and lunged at the girl, unleashing his best skill—but it was like his sword betrayed him, twisting out of the girl's way.

She had a dagger in each hand.

Even as she dodged, she slashed his arm with both of them.

"Gah!"

And as he flinched, she put the book in her inventory, then promptly ran off.

"C-come back here!"

He ran after her, heedless of the damage spray—but an instant later, red sparks gushed from his guts like fresh blood...and then he vanished in a burst of light.

The girl he'd been chasing had disappeared—and she was standing where he'd fallen, spinning her daggers.

"You really shouldn't fall for the same trick twice."

"Huh? I...wh-what the—?"

The sole survivor couldn't process any of this. He was just sputtering, at a total loss.

And in that condition...

There was no way he could ever beat Sally.

"Bye-bye, now."

A moment later, the last player transformed into light.

Sally didn't know where the three of them had started out, but she was confident they had no way of getting their book back.

"If you can't beat me...you definitely aren't beating Maple."

Maple came running up to her.

"See? Told you it would work."

"Yeah! It was fun seeing you break character."

"That wasn't the point!"

"Do it again! Especially the part where you started skipping."

"No! Never again! Focus on the spoils!"

"...Fine, I'll let you off the hook *this* time."

"...Good. Argh, that was *so* not me."

Sally vowed never to act like that again, no matter how effective it might be.

They started rummaging through everything the players had dropped.

◆□◆□◆□◆□◆

Their first bit of loot was also their main goal: the book.

Additionally, they were rewarded with three medals after the fight.

That was definitely a stroke of luck.

Anyone who'd found three medals would likely avoid high-level opponents like the plague.

If Sally had been in her usual gear, they'd probably have bolted at the first sight of her. Maybe not everyone would notice, but Sally's equipment definitely didn't look like anything they sold in shops.

And the fact that she had five medals—more than the three of them—had definitely robbed them of their better judgment.

Who could resist the chance to almost triple their medals?

"You play with fire, ya gonna get burned." Sally chuckled. Then she took the old book out of her inventory. "Let's give this a look-see."

"Yeah, I'm definitely curious."

They sat down on the wall, peering at the pages.

It was in such poor condition, almost nothing was legible. But when she flipped through it, she found one page with a readable passage.

"The Ancient Heart—guided by gushing water and the beckoning faint light…there did I spy it. If thou dost have the courage to dispel evil, then hasten to the quiet azure depths."

"What does *that* mean?"

"This Ancient Heart's got something to do with this water… and that leads you to a dungeon? Seems like there'll be a fight, too."

"…Water… Is there a fountain, or…?"

Sure enough, a quick check of the area led them to four fountains.

There was a big one in the center of all the dilapidated ruins and three little ones placed some distance away.

At the top of each fountain was a diamond-shaped red crystal with a lovely gleam.

But all the fountains were dried up—no water anywhere.

"Let's start with the big one in the middle."

"Sounds like a plan."

It was a short walk to the fountain.

Sally climbed up into the fountain's main basin. Clearly, she had an idea.

"Oceanic!"

Water gushed out from her feet.

The basin was quickly filled to the brim.

As soon as it was, the entire fountain took on a faint blue glow.

"Ohhh!"

"Nice!"

But the glow soon faded.

The water in the basin vanished, like the fountain had absorbed it.

They listened closely, but it didn't sound like anything had activated.

"Hmm. Nothing's happening…"

"…No. But there's clearly something up with this fountain."

"Totally. Let's try the others, too."

They repeated this at all the fountains. Each of them glowed briefly, but nothing more.

*   *   *

"If the faint light is these glowing fountains…do we need the water to gush?"

Thinking about it wasn't getting them anywhere, so they tabled the discussion and looked through the book again.

"Oh!"

"A drawing?"

There was something on the last page.

This, too, was in poor condition, but they could just make out the illustration on it.

"Pots…or jugs?"

People were placing some sort of vessels around the four fountains. Something round was floating at the top of the picture. This was painted red.

"Is that the Ancient Heart?" Maple asked, pointing at the red blob.

"…Maybe? Hmm. Do we have to fill some jugs and place them around the fountains? I don't get it."

They both made a lot of thinking noises, but the picture was too abstract, and no clear plans emerged.

"Let's take a break. We clearly aren't getting anywhere."

"It sure doesn't feel like we are, no."

They sat down in the center of the ruins. Not even trying to hide. It was easier to relax with a clear view of all approaches.

"Only three more days left…counting today," Sally mused.

They were well past the halfway point. Only a little time left.

"I feel like these past four days have been suuuuuuuuuuper packed! Like, way more stuff happened than in all the rest of the time we've played combined."

"Ah-ha-ha, yeah, maybe."

They'd beaten a goblin king, spent the night in a haunted forest, gone up against a stupidly powerful bird on a mountaintop, made friends with Syrup and Oboro, and explored a moonlit bamboo thicket.

Then they'd fought fake versions of each other in a canyon, met Kasumi in the desert, and been chased by snails through an endless cave.

Finally, they'd met Kanade on the beach, getting new medals and a new friend.

Like Maple said, the event had been jam-packed.

"If we can finish these ruins…and a dungeon, if there is one, I'll be done for the day."

"So we spend the rest of the day here?"

"Yeah, let's go with that. It might just take us that long…"

That finished their break, and they got up to explore the ruins some more.

They split up to cover more ground and checked every corner, but by the time the sun set, they'd still found nothing.

"What now? Keep looking?"

"It might be time dependent, and…we need to be ready for tomorrow. So I'd say we take turns sleeping while the other one explores."

"Works for me!"

They'd traded shifts several times. It was currently Maple's turn to explore.

"Good luck!"

"Yeah…I hope I find something."

Maple set off into the ruins once more.

She started with the fountain. Each shift, that was where she'd gone first.

Then she'd check the smaller fountains around it.

Then she'd look up at the sky.

"The moon really is beautiful…"

There was a full moon tonight, its pale light casting a soft glow on the ground.

The real world had artificial light everywhere, and Maple had never realized how much light the moon gave off.

She was almost at the fountain again.

"Mm-hmm?"

Maple stopped in her tracks.

This was the change they'd been waiting for.

The fountain was glowing. Without either of them doing anything.

Maple quickly sent Sally a message.

Sally caught up with her in less than a minute.

"Wow! It's totally glowing."

"Yeah! I figured that was an important sign."

Sally hopped up on the basin and used Oceanic again.

"The glow got brighter…but not enough."

Once again, it had simply absorbed all the water.

Sally hung her head, dejected.

Maple thought about this for a moment, until an idea suddenly hit her.

"What if it needs to be all of them at once? I mean, there are four fountains."

"That makes sense, but…we couldn't get to them all in time. Even with Superspeed, I'm not *that* fast."

"But we're not getting anywhere as is, so…why not try?"

"Try what?"

"You're not the only one who can make a liquid, Sally."

Maple explained her plan.

"Uh…huh. That…might be worth a shot."

Sally hopped back up on the basin and activated Oceanic.

Just before she did, Maple yelled, "Hydra!"

Poison was *technically* a liquid.

And the Hydra had *three* heads.

She had each of them point at a different smaller fountain and swallow it up.

Maple's plan was a total shot in the dark, but it turned out that fortune was on their side.

"Whoa!"

"That's really bright!"

The three smaller fountains each shot a beam of light at the main one.

The big fountain's glow grew brighter and brighter, and the red crystal levitated.

The crystal began gathering moonlight, becoming even brighter, bathing the whole area in red…and then it shattered.

"Um."

"Wh-what now?"

They looked around nervously…and then there was a rumble behind them.

It echoed through the quiet ruins—and both girls spun around.

"What…the…?"

"Whoa…!"

What had once been the main street sprang up at the fountain steps...

...and ran all the way to the cliff-top prominence.

To the pedestal and the standing stones.

Even from this distance, they could see a glowing white light.

The rumble had been the sound of the pedestal and standing stones...crumbling.

They moved closer to examine the new glow. It was a magic circle—they'd seen plenty of those by now.

Careful not to step on it, they moved around, inspecting where the standing stones had been.

And found...

"Yikes."

"S-spooky..."

The sea below them had parted. There was now a dark pit, so deep that they could not see the bottom.

"I bet there's something down there..."

"Yeah, basically guaranteed. Maple, wanna jump?"

"N-nope, nope, can't, won't. Too scary!"

It was the middle of the night.

The ocean at night was always sinister, and jumping into the creepiest part of it took more courage than Maple had, even if she *might* be able to soak up the damage.

"Then...guess we'd better take the magic circle. It probably connects to the bottom."

"Somewhere nobody else has explored."

"Yup."

On the count of three, both girls hopped onto the circle.

And once again, their bodies turned to light.

"So dark!"

"Sally? I can't even see you!"

"Hang on a second."

Sally took a lamp out of her inventory and lit it.

"Are we…underwater?"

"Oh! Look up!"

Sally did and saw stars above.

"We're definitely at the bottom of that pit."

"There's a path going that way!"

The passage was a perfect half circle.

The walls were made entirely of water.

Some mysterious power was keeping the ocean at bay, form-ing a path.

"Let's hurry through. Don't want this collapsing on us."

"Yeah! That would be bad."

They made haste through the darkened underwater tunnel.

By the light of day, this might well be genuinely beautiful—but since this could happen only at night, no one would ever know.

The lamp's feeble light was not enough to keep their fears at bay. Before they knew it, the girls were holding hands.

"Oh! There's light up ahead!"

"Wh-whew!"

They ran even faster. The light grew bigger, and by the time they reached it—it was taller than either of them.

The light came from the ocean.

It was like time flowed differently here—this space was as bright as day.

They could hear bubbles rising as fish happily swam about.

It pushed back the darkness, banishing their fears.

And there was a single staircase, made of coral, stretching through the daylit sea.

At the top was a door, also coral. They'd seen doors like this before. That led…to a boss room.

"'Dispel evil…' Ready for a fight?"

"Yup! Anytime."

Maple raised her shield, showing how ready she was.

Sally took a deep breath…and opened the door.

"Maple, it's a domed room, well lit. Kinda the same as this one."

"Aha!"

"And, uh…it's big. Like, over fifty yards across. Ceiling's pretty high, too."

"Then…the boss is big, too?"

Big bosses usually came in big boss rooms.

"Floor's dry stone…for now. Don't see any traps."

"Got it. On your mark?"

"Go!"

"Here we go!"

They leaped through the door.

Not wanting to waste Devour, Maple didn't hold up her shield.

Like Sally said, there were no traps. No physical attacks that would deplete her stock of Devour.

"……………! Here it comes!"

"Yup!"

There was a splash, and several tentacles emerged from the ceiling above.

These were clearly squid arms.

"Is it *that* dungeon?!"

"But this one isn't underwater!"

As they gaped, the giant squid attacked.

Tentacles as big as the girls swung at Maple.

"Fine...not fine?!"

Her great shield swallowed up a squid tentacle, but the HP bar above didn't budge.

Not because it had a lot of health.

She simply hadn't done any damage.

"We might have to attack the main body to do anything!"

"Whaaaat?!"

"This...is gonna suck," Sally muttered, glancing up at the squid swimming above.

The squid didn't care what she thought. It just kept attacking from the comfort and safety of the sea outside.

CHAPTER 10

Defense Build and the Squid Hunt

Thirty minutes into the battle…

"Okay…what else can we try…?"

"Sally! Any ideas?"

"Uh…not yet…"

Sally was standing stock-still, lost in thought.

This was possible because the tentacles were entirely focused on Maple.

Maple was getting slapped silly.

"Thank god your defense is so ridiculous."

These attacks would one-shot any other player, or at least put them in the red, but they didn't hurt Maple any more than a bunny's tackle.

Maple was currently flying through the air like a pinball.

"Maple! I'm gonna try swimming up to it!"

"Got it! Be careful!"

Sally had already run through her spell collection, but none of them had managed to penetrate the thick layer of water protecting the squid.

Maple had suggested using Hydra to poison the water itself, but if that didn't work, it would still leave the water too poisonous for Sally to swim around. They'd decided to make that idea their last resort.

First, Sally was going to swim up to it.

But not *all* the tentacles were busy slapping Maple.

It had kept a couple in reserve for any threats that got too close.

Naturally, these immediately closed in on Sally.

"Wow...nice, Sally."

Sailing through the air after another tentacle hit, Maple looked up and saw Sally deftly threading the gaps between the tentacles, steadily drawing closer to the boss's body.

"Oh! The HP bar actually budged!"

Sally's daggers had lit up with the attack effect, slicing into the squid. Maple watched, enduring more blows.

"Hmm...it has less HP than I feared..."

Sally did a five-skill combo, and that alone chewed through 15 percent of the boss's health bar.

"Mm?!"

The tentacles around Maple stopped attacking, and she went crashing to the ground.

Sally dealing a decent chunk of damage had drawn the tentacle's aggro away from Maple.

Realizing this, Sally quickly swam back to her friend.

No matter how good you were at dodging, a proper AOE would still hit you.

And if all those tentacles swung together, she'd be done for.

"Gasp..."

"Cover Move! Cover!"

Maple didn't use Devour. She just jumped between Sally and the tentacles and let them all clang against her armor.

"Hydra!"

The poison dragon swallowed up all eight tentacles.

This squid was nowhere near as fast as the bird, so the Hydra landed its hits easily, without needing any tricks or special timing.

It simply wasn't fast enough to dodge.

"But they grow back."

They could take out the tentacles, but they soon respawned without any effect on the boss's main health.

It wasn't entirely pointless, though. It did get them to focus on Maple again.

"Sally, you're up!"

"Thanks! You're a life saver!"

Sally swam back out into the ocean.

Sally attacked, and Maple drew the aggro.

Each time the boss started targeting Sally, she came back to Maple, and Maple made herself the target again.

They just had to rinse and repeat until something changed.

Phase two arrived sooner than expected.

When Sally had carved its health down to 70 percent, the boss changed things up.

Magic circles appeared all around the squid, generating fish.

These were clearly monsters.

The fish monsters swam toward the two girls.

All the tentacles that had been busy with Maple lost interest in her, withdrawing into the water.

"They're swimming in air!"

Maple wasn't underwater, but the fish didn't seem to care. They were jumping right out of the ocean and soaring effortlessly through the air—coated in a blue aura.

It was rather pretty, but...they were still monsters. She couldn't exactly stop and stare.

Fish were slamming into Maple from all directions.

"Hmm...Paralyze Shout!"

A *schiiing* echoed through the chamber, and the fish all fell to the floor, unable to move.

"This is so good!" Maple cried.

But the squid and any fish still in the water were out of range, leaving them all unaffected.

"*Gasp!* I got away somehow!" Sally said. She emerged from the water, dripping.

The rest of the fish and all the tentacles were right on her heels.

But Sally was acting like she'd already gotten away—because Maple was there.

There were few places in the world safer than next to Maple.

"Maple!"

"Gotcha!"

Maple drew New Moon again.

A purple sigil appeared at its tip.

Maple's favorite—and most powerful—attack.

"Hydra!"

It melted all the approaching fish, and swallowed up the tentacles beyond, and...

...plunged into the water.

""Augh!""

Every one of the Hydra's heads was well inside the water, where they dissolved.

Were they imagining it, or had the ocean taken on a faint purple tint?

They weren't sure if Sally could safely swim through that.

"N-n-n-now what?!"

"D-d-don't ask me!"

"Um, uh, right! The squid! Its health bar!"

She looked up…and its health bar wasn't going down at all.

The tentacles were regenerating.

The fish she'd paralyzed were getting that blue aura around them and taking off again.

New fish were still spawning.

"I—I guess you'd better start running, Sally?"

"I'll take out a few fish as I do!"

"Super sorry!"

So many fish.

Eight flailing tentacles.

And those fish could do more than just tackle. They were spraying water the same color as their glowing aura.

"Maple! I think that's like Oceanic!"

This was a skill Sally had that reduced her opponent's Agility, and she was pretty sure these fish could do the same thing.

"I already got hit! But…I'm not getting any slower?"

"W-well, no. You never had any Agility! You can't get less than zero! Or…maybe it is just normal water? Argh, I don't know anymore!"

Maple's blunder had put a stop to their reliable strategy, and now there was poison and mystery fish fluid all over the floor. The air was filling with fish and wriggly tentacles.

Maple was in full pinball mode.

Between screams of panic, they were both yelling ideas the moment they came to mind, and it was the epitome of utter pandemonium.

◆□◆□◆□◆□◆

"To hell with it! See how much poison you can dump in the ocean!"

"Right! Then just let me Devour some of these tentacles!"

"Go for it!"

Maple's shield promptly swallowed up some of the squid's limbs.

Each time it did, a red crystal appeared on the surface.

This was her MP reserve.

"While Maple handles the squid—I'm gonna catch me some fish."

Sally headed into the swarm, always at top speed, doing her usual hit and run.

Meanwhile, Maple…

"Right. Let's hope this works!"

She was standing by the ocean wall.

She'd just swallowed up all the tentacles, so she had bought herself a few moments of relative peace.

Fish were still tackling her, but she simply ignored them.

"Wow, from close up, they're kinda cute!"

Maple reached out toward one of the fish, only for it to tackle her hand.

But she was all smiles, so it looked less like a monster attack and more like a kid playing with their pet fish.

"You should probably back off now," Maple said and pointed New Moon at the water. "Hydra!"

She didn't aim at anything in particular, so the Hydra just hurtled into the ocean depths.

And naturally, its body dissolved in the water, doing no direct damage to the squid.

"May the beautiful ocean...turn to poison!" Maple called out in a singsong voice.

There was a lot of water, and she'd clearly have to keep attacking.

But the water was definitely taking on an increasingly purple hue. It was much more obvious than before.

"Better move away from the wall so the tentacles don't knock me in."

Maple moved to the center of the dome, splashing through the poison she'd created and the water the fish had sprayed.

She had to wait a bit before she could use Hydra again.

And that gave the tentacles time to regenerate.

Since Sally wasn't attacking the squid at all, its attention was focused entirely on Maple.

"Go on! Do your worst!" she said, lying down on the ground.

She figured there was no escaping her pinball fate, so she might as well not even bother resisting.

"Oh?"

But when she lay down, the tentacles were just slapping her uselessly from above.

They couldn't get any lift like they had when she was upright.

"Nice! This is way better."

"Yikes... This is nuts, even for her..."

Sally was busy running a marathon with a school of fish chasing after her, so...she was hardly one to talk.

*   *   *

Maple spent a while dumping poison in the ocean.

And both girls noticed the squid's HP was starting to slowly drain.

"It's going!"

"I think so! But..."

There was a looooong gap between each visible drop.

Like, five whole minutes. And each of those took maybe a millimeter off its health bar.

If they had to wait that long, it would quickly become actively painful.

"Keep going!"

"I will!"

A few more Hydras and the HP drain grew visibly faster.

An hour later, she'd succeeded in carving off 10 percent.

The boss had 60 percent health remaining.

At this rate, they'd be fighting for another six hours.

"Poison Lance!"

Maple had run out of ammo for Hydra, so she started using other skills.

"Six more hours of running like this is a bit much!"

"What do we do?"

Nothing she could think of seemed like it would make a dramatic difference.

They went on like this for another hour, and the squid's health dropped below 50 percent.

"Yikes!"

Maple had been lying down near the water wall, so she noticed right away.

The water was expanding.

The walls and ceiling drew closer.

When they finally stopped, the space in the dome had shrunk to half its original size.

Then the squid itself spewed a cloud of ink, hiding itself in the water.

It had been hard enough moving around in the water before, and doing so blind? Fighting this thing the proper way would've been *really* hard.

But since they'd already given up on the legitimate approach…

"Maple, how many Devour left?"

"Just one!"

"…Save it."

"Roger!"

With the walls closing in, the fish attacks were coming at them more quickly.

Which made it much harder for Sally to run.

"Taunt!"

If Sally was struggling, then they were better off having Maple draw their aggro. She made herself a big target.

"Thanks!"

"No prob."

The squid wasn't spraying ink constantly—just as Maple's poison was diluted, so was the ink.

They could now see it swimming gracefully around, like it had no plans for a second ink cloud.

"There it is… I think it's in range? Okay! Maple!"

Maple hopped to her feet and came over.

"What's the plan?"

"Come with me! Leap!"

Her jump took her toward the squid, but she was still a good fifteen yards off.

"Cover Move!" Maple yelled, following Sally's lead.

"Here goes! Shoulder Throw!"

Sally grabbed Maple and yanked her into a throw, flinging her toward the water.

"Aiiiieeeeee?!"

"Impact Fist!"

Sally threw a punch. There was a *crack*, and a projectile made of air hit Maple, pushing her higher—through the water above.

Maple went rocketing directly toward the squid, swinging her great shield.

Which immediately took a huge bite of its health the moment they came into contact.

"I call it the Maple Cannon!"

"H-how am I supposed to land?!"

".........I didn't think that far ahead."

They'd been exploring a long time and then had a very long fight—and Sally wasn't really thinking as clearly anymore.

Maple was doomed to hit the ground with a very loud *clang*.

"Since *I* did a ton of damage...," Sally said, landing softly.

Maple crashed down next to her.

A good twenty-five-yard fall...from which she took no damage. Incredible endurance.

Meanwhile, the squid didn't seem to have much in the way of HP or defense.

The way Sally's attacks had torn it up early on proved that.

She'd figured if they could land one of Maple's big hits, then a single blow could easily knock off 20 percent or more.

"That saved us a good three hours!"

"But that still leaves *another* three."

Maple was all out of Devour. They couldn't pull that trick a second time.

"Oh, there goes the ink again."

"And to think how nice this ocean used to look."

Between the ink and the poison, there were no pretty blue patches left.

The girls held out until the boss's HP broke the 10 percent mark.

And it entered its final phase.

"Huh? The fish are…"

The fish lost their auras…and then they dried up, turning to dust.

The auras themselves rose upward and were absorbed into the squid boss.

"Brace yourself!"

"I am!"

Maple had her shield up.

She was out of Devour, so she could finally use it like a regular shield.

The giant squid shook itself; then a blue aura enveloped it—just like had happened to the fish. It shot out of the water…

And the powerful blue glow kept its massive bulk aloft.

"Incoming!"

"Cover Move! Cover!"

As Maple yelled, the squid hit them.

Maple had covered her just in case, and while she was being flung around and was soaking up the squid's onslaught, Sally was able to safely dodge away.

The squid kept going, plunging into the water on the far side of the dome.

It had taken a good 40 percent of Maple's health with it.

Cover Move doubled the damage she took.

But this was only the second time Sally had seen anything with a high enough damage output to punch through Maple's defenses with brute force.

"One hell of a buff," Sally muttered.

She cast Heal on Maple, keeping one eye on the squid.

If it was coming in to attack them, that would open it up to a potential counter.

"Dodge...and strike!" Sally yelled.

The squid's attention was fully on Maple.

"Superspeed!"

And that meant it was open to Sally's attacks.

Going into slo-mo, she swung her daggers.

"Triple Slash!"

Six blows struck its underbelly as Sally slid beneath it.

"Poison Lance!"

Maple stabbed it right in the head.

The squid's attack hurt Maple, but it took more damage than she did.

It splashed into the water on the far side.

*   *   *

"We'll finish it next time!"

"It's almost toast! Hang in there!"

They followed it closely with their eyes, ready to go again.

Not wanting to blow their best opportunity.

The squid wheeled toward them, ready for another charge.

"Here it comes!"

"Yeah!"

They hefted their weapons…

…and the last of the squid's health fell victim to poison.

""Huh?!""

It turned to light, vanishing.

The light cleansed the water.

The particles sparkled like sunlight, rocking in the currents, and slowly faded out.

"…………Well, that was anticlimactic."

"…………You can say that again."

Neither of them had found that victory at all satisfying.

Still, a win was a win. A deep-blue magic circle appeared in front of them.

"Hop on?"

"Is there a reward?"

"Uh…there might be? Should I go swim around a bit?"

"Please do."

Sally dived in.

The poison was gone, and she could explore to her heart's content.

"If only Syrup were a sea turtle, I could've asked it to help."

But all she could do was watch Sally swim around until she came back.

"Just one squid tentacle."

"No medals?"

"Uh…not any that I could find. I searched among the coral pretty thoroughly. And I doubt the rewards would drop somewhere *that* hard to find."

"True…"

But no medals was still disappointing. They stepped onto the magic circle.

They'd just assumed this would take them to the cliff above so were shocked to find themselves underwater.

"H-how will I breathe?! This is bad!"

"Uh, wait. Maple! We *can* breathe."

"Huh? Oh. You're right…"

Both of them were talking normally.

They could feel the water all around them but weren't drowning.

"How mysterious!"

"Is this the 'quiet azure depths'?"

It certainly was quiet.

If they kept silent, the only audible sound was the occasional bubble.

This seemed to be the seafloor but fairly near the surface.

The still of the blue around them was almost soporific—but there was a blue treasure chest cradled in the coral.

"Mind if I do the honors?"

Inside were two medals and two scrolls.

Sally picked up the scroll and read the description.

"What skill is it?"

"Ancient Ocean. The prereq is a water skill...lets you summon those blue aura fish from earlier."

They'd seen more than enough of those during the squid battle.

Sally read further. Like she'd suspected, their blue water attack was a 10 percent Agility debuff.

This wasn't a skill that would help Maple out much, but it would give Sally more options.

They'd solved the puzzle on the surface to get here. That had weakened the boss and changed the rewards for victory—but they had no way of knowing that.

"Uh...does Hydra count?"

"I'm gonna go out on a limb and say that's *not* a water skill, no."

"Figured."

Maple gave it a shot but was unable to acquire the skill.

So she put the skill in her inventory, saving it for another day.

They closed the chest and lay down.

It had been a long battle, and they'd done a lot of exploring in the ruins. They were both exhausted.

And they'd met Kanade earlier that morning.

It really had been a very busy day.

"Maybe it wouldn't hurt to spend *one* day relaxing."

"Ah-ha-ha...maybe not."

If they reached their medal goal in time, maybe they could take the seventh day off.

For the moment, they simply went to sleep. This was the perfect spot for a nap.

"Let's just…rest awhile…"

"Yeah…"

The sea's embrace made this the best bed they'd found yet.

CHAPTER 11

Defense Build and the Event's Sixth Day

After a while, they got back up.

This time, the magic circle took them to the cliff top.

The ruins lay behind them.

Meanwhile, the pit in the sea below was gone.

"So we're done here, then?"

"Yup. But it wasn't enough medals…"

"Oh. Riiight. We still need two more."

They'd slept in a bit. It was now nine in the morning on the sixth day.

"If there are any dungeons that still haven't been cleared… they'll be pretty tough or extremely hard to find."

"Yeah…either way, we'd better get moving."

Maple turned to walk away, but Sally stopped her.

"Maple—you're out of Devour, right?"

"Erp…did the date change while we were busy fighting the squid?"

If she didn't have her Devour stock back, Maple wouldn't be much use in a serious fight.

Sally pondered this a moment and then offered a suggestion.

*　　*　　*

"This leaves us no choice. We *have* to target other players."

"Hngg… All right, fine."

Sally was definitely way more enthusiastic about PKing than Maple, but if the choice came down to hunt or be hunted, she could make her peace with it.

A lot of the players they'd met so far *had* tried to take them down.

And that fact helped convince Maple this was their best option.

"Then…into the woods we go. Maple? See that mountain?"

"Huh? Yeah, but…"

"Let's head that way. I figure a landmark like that'll lure in other players."

This was not the same mountain they'd climbed their second day.

It definitely seemed like the kind of mountain that would have a dungeon inside, but since it really drew the eye, odds were the dungeon had already been cleared.

"Works for me."

With that decided, they set out.

Three hours later.

They were in a cave at the base of the mountain.

They'd seen other players on their way here, but they'd all run for it.

And with Maple's combat potential at rock bottom, Sally didn't want to risk leaving her to give chase.

"Does that make sense? You mind hiding here, Maple?"

"No prob! Also…sorry?"

"No need for that! You did well in the squid fight."

Sally pulled up her menu and then handed her ring to Maple.

This was the ring that connected her to Oboro.

"It'll cost you some HP, but…Oboro can help guard you."

Maple removed her Toughness Ring and put Sally's on. Then she summoned both pet monsters.

"Cool…then I'll go do what I can!"

"Good luck out there!"

Sally dashed out of the cave.

They hadn't trained Syrup and Oboro much, but the monsters could handle lower-level players. Maybe even the middle of the mid-tier.

And that made them decent enough bodyguards.

If Maple died, they'd lose all the medals they'd gathered.

"And that's a grave responsibility… Oh, I know!"

There might be no boss room left, but this cave had been a dungeon once, so it was fairly big.

One of those ant-farm-like sprawls.

And Maple was at the very bottom of it.

"Venom Capsule!"

Wary of friendly fire, she'd put Syrup and Oboro away first. Then she hid herself inside a poison capsule, gradually increasing the size.

This was a skill Maple could use even without Devour.

"I've gotta survive till Sally comes back!"

As much as her MP recovery allowed, she expanded the capsule, gradually filling the cave passage.

The dungeon quickly changed into a poison swamp.

It was like Maple had transformed herself into the new dungeon boss.

"Keep your distance! None may enter here!"

Maple expanded her capsule yet again.

*　　*　　*

While Maple was gushing poison, Sally was outside the cave.

"On my own...there should be a lot of players I can take out."

Far too many players recognized Maple on sight.

This was why those players earlier had bolted—one look at Maple, and they'd been in the wind.

Everyone knew just how dangerous she could be.

But not Sally.

She was entirely unknown.

Sally was every bit as broken as Maple and far more aggressive.

But only a few players were aware of this.

And Sally had nothing to lose.

Maple was holding all their medals.

"Been a while...but I'm in the mood for a proper rampage."

Sally enjoyed teaming up with Maple, but solo fights brought their own thrills.

She raced off down the mountain.

It was just past noon. Visibility was high.

"Aha! Got some."

Sally found two women walking in the woods, one with a spear and one with a sword. They were paying attention and spotted Sally right away.

"Incoming!"

"I see her!"

The sword wielder had a shield equipped and started edging closer, guard up.

"Gale Thrust!"

The spear wielder drove her weapon in Sally's direction, but Sally saw it coming and was already one step ahead.

Her opponent had seen her daggers, assumed she'd dodge the thrust, and planned to strike while Sally was off-balance.

This was a solid plan.

Your average player would step back or dodge to one side.

The spear wielder had bet on the former and followed the thrust with a dash forward, closing the gap.

This was the best choice—even if Sally had dodged sideways, she could still easily handle that.

But Sally was not an average player.

"Huh?!"

Sally didn't dodge like ordinary people.

She twisted her body *just* enough to avoid the blow and kept moving forward. The spear wielder was left wide open, and Sally's daggers closed in.

"Double Slash!"

Red sparks flew, but the spear wielder still lived.

And she was already swinging her spear sideways.

"You're kidding?!"

Sally dodged *this* by limboing under it. It was hard to believe any human could react that fast—and the shock made the spear wielder's mind go blank.

"And you're done."

Sally's daggers brought the spear wielder's HP to zero.

"Power Blade!"

A swift vertical strike from Sally's rear.

The sword wielder was sure she'd gotten her.

"...............!"

But Sally turned like she had eyes in the back of her head.

A small pivot let the blow sail harmlessly past, as if the blade were avoiding Sally.

"Slash!"

Sally sped past the sword wielder, striking her in the flank.

The sword wielder found this all very unsettling.

It was like the more she attacked, the worse things got for her.

"Argh…"

"Wind Cutter!"

And while she scowled at Sally, trying to figure out how to land a blow—well, she hadn't expected her to use *magic*, too.

Perhaps this was a sign she was starting to panic.

"Ah!"

She leaped to one side, avoiding the spell.

But this was exactly the position they'd tried to put Sally in. She realized as much, but too late to recover her balance.

"Good-bye."

Face-to-face, typical players stood little chance against anyone genuinely skilled.

And no miracles arrived to save them.

"Right, no medals, then."

Sally set out in search of her next prey.

As luck would have it, the sixth day had brought many players to this area.

Afterward, those players all gave the same testimony.

"She vanished like an illusion."

"My blade avoided her."

"Was she ever there at all?"

*   *   *

This was how the slaughter began—and in time, this carnage would come to be known as the Sixth Day Nightmare.

◆□◆□◆□◆□◆

"Hokay…time to head back," Sally said, face lit by the red sparks of a dying player.

If this game had blood instead of particle effects, her beautiful blue equipment would have been stained crimson long ago.

In days to come, some victims would speculate that she'd actually been a powerful field boss that spawned out of nowhere, but for now, her reign of terror drew to a close.

Because her kills had earned her two medals.

"Not many people have any, huh? Were we just lucky, or…?"

The sun was already setting.

She could see the mountain where Maple waited, silhouetted against the sunset.

It was a good six miles away.

Sally had quit counting after she killed her hundredth victim.

Yet she had only two medals to show for it.

Sally's suspicions were correct—they had been very fortunate.

But what had really made a difference was that the girls had been strong enough to clear the dungeons they found.

"Just gotta get these back safely."

Sally broke into a run.

She came upon several players on her way and turned them to light—but that was just their lot in life.

*   *   *

"Phew, made it!"

Sally stepped into the cave.

She knew the way, so she'd started quickly weaving through the maze toward Maple's location…only to stop in her tracks halfway.

"Yikes…"

The passage before her was blocked by a wall of poison.

Attacking that would just leave the floor covered in poison, so Sally wasn't going any farther.

"That's definitely Maple… Guess I'd better message her."

She sent one off and waited a bit. Eventually, Maple emerged from the poison.

"I found two medals!" Sally said.

"Wow! That's great."

Sally tossed them over to Maple.

They finally had twenty.

All they had to do now was keep it that way.

"What's the plan? We've got our medals, so we can kick back and train these two the rest of the event."

"Oh! That reminds me! I had an idea that might help with that."

"What?"

"Come with me!"

"Uh…I literally can't…"

Sally pointed to the poison-drenched floor.

"Oh…uh, want a shield ride?"

Maple canceled her capsule, and the poison wall vanished. Then she put her great shield down on the floor.

"Okay, but how does this work?"

Sally sat down on the shield like it was a sled.

"I'm gonna push it."

"Um."

"I'm gonna push it!"

"I don't think that'll work."

"Trust me—it'll work!"

Maple gave it a push.

It moved maybe twenty inches before coming to a complete halt.

"…It didn't work."

"That's what I was afraid of. Anyway, what's your idea? Let's start with that."

"Well, um…so there's a dead end—not the one you left me in—and there were ant monsters in it that were only, like, eight inches tall. And they were really weak! I thought they'd be perfect for Syrup and Oboro."

They hadn't checked the cave out very thoroughly before, so this was news to Sally.

Maple had gotten bored, so once she was safe behind the poison, she'd gone out exploring and found the ants.

"They spawn continuously?" Sally asked.

If they did, then that *would* be a good place to train them.

"Three every ten minutes!"

"Then…you wanna take care of it, Maple? I'm clearly not getting there anytime soon."

"Okay! Leave it to me!"

Sally got off the shield, and Maple reequipped it. Then she headed back into the cave's depths.

"Hmm…but now I've got nothing else to do," Sally said.

She walked back to the cave entrance.

It wasn't like the whole place was contaminated with poison. Just a third of it.

Sally settled down in an open chamber not too far from the entrance.

It was a square room, maybe twenty yards on each side, with decorations lining the walls.

Sally assumed it had once been home to a mid-boss.

"Guess I'll just guard Maple."

This wasn't a dungeon you had to take a magic circle to reach.

And because it had long since been cleared, the monster spawn rate was pretty low.

Just a few routine spawns like the one Maple had found.

And Sally didn't know where those were.

So what was she protecting Maple from?

Certainly not monsters. No, she was guarding against other players.

There were so few dungeons left that players would come looking for medals in anything that looked even remotely dungeon-like.

"And if one of them has Poison Nullification, she's sunk."

Without Devour, Maple had no way to beat a player with that skill and decent defense.

Since Sally had nothing better to do, she'd decided to guard against that possibility.

"That makes this…kinda like a dungeon…"

Maple was the boss, and Sally was the mid-boss—and twenty medals were up for grabs if any players could clear it.

And almost no monsters.

A special dungeon.

*　　*　　*

"Just gotta keep her safe until the sixth day ends..."

Once the seventh day started, Maple would return to full strength. If they could last that long, Maple would be reviiiiived!

"That makes Maple sound like a dark god..."

Given how many players had been clustered near this mountain, Sally wondered if there was anything left to explore in regions beyond.

"Did they come here because all the other areas have been picked clean?"

As Sally mused, she heard voices coming down the passage.

"Something up ahead!"

A party of four entered, weapons at the ready.

Sally quickly noted each.

A spear, a great shield, a wand, and a greatsword.

Looked like they played together regularly. Solid party balance.

"Who goes there?" she growled.

"Are you...a player? Or..."

She was lurking in the mid-boss room, covered head to toe in top-notch gear—unsurprisingly, it was a little hard to be sure.

They could see her health bar, but that was also true for monsters.

If Sally claimed to be a monster, they might actually buy it.

"Looking for a fight?"

If they knew she was a player, they'd want her medals and would probably attack. Even if Sally told the truth—she didn't have any—they had no reason to believe that.

And they were clearly here to explore, so if she let them pass, they'd find the poison halls Maple had left behind.

And that would convince them this dungeon had not yet been cleared.

And if they were capable of getting through those—Maple was in trouble.

Taking them out was the safest bet.

Plus, it might be fun to *act* like she was a monster.

So Sally had decided to speak in clichés.

"Mid-boss! Score!"

Convinced by her act, the party members were certain they'd found an uncleared dungeon.

"Try to entertain me!" Sally said, spawning blue aura fish around her.

The real reason she was role-playing a monster…

…was because her recent reign of terror had left her high on adrenaline.

She wasn't ready to quit fighting just yet.

And if they thought she was a monster—they would definitely throw everything they had at her.

She figured she had to take 'em out either way, so she might as well enjoy it.

Enjoying herself was what gaming was all about.

"Heh-heh-heh…what a treat!"

"Careful! Incoming!"

"""Ah!"""

Games had pleasures the real world could never offer.

And that was true for both Sally and the party she was up against.

Meanwhile, Maple was lying on the floor in a room at the back, cheering on Syrup and Oboro.

*   *   *

"Snap! Get 'em! Keep trying! Fox Fire!"

The ants died, and Maple smiled approvingly.

"Good, good! Keep this up and you'll be stronger in no time!"

She sat up, petting both monsters.

If she wasn't wearing full armor, she'd have just looked like a normal kid playing with her pet animals.

Something seen all the time out in the real world.

Maple had no idea Sally was locked in mortal combat at that very moment.

Then again, perhaps Maple was the real exception here.

She played with Syrup and Oboro for a while.

Frolicking and cuddling didn't exactly help boost their levels, but Maple had fun.

"All right, enough running around... You always catch me—because this room is very small. Mm-hmm, that's definitely the only reason."

Maple sat down heavily, intently watching Syrup as it walked around.

A few minutes later, the monsters respawned.

"Oh, they're back! Taunt! Syrup, use Snap. Oboro, Fox Fire!"

Maple stayed seated but used her Taunt skill to pull the enemy toward her.

And while the monsters gnawed on her ineffectively, the two pets attacked from behind.

"Go on! Keep it up! Once more! Snap! Fox Fire!"

Under Maple's watchful eye, Syrup and Oboro successfully defeated the ant monsters.

"And that's a level-up! Woo! Heh-heh. You're so good! Oh, you both learned new skills!"

Maple showered them with praise and pets.

She knew this didn't affect their stats, but she *wanted* to be affectionate.

"Out in the real world, it's a lot harder to play with cute animals like you, Syrup. Eh-heh-heh! You're both adorable."

Training their pets might have been Maple's job, but that didn't mean she couldn't enjoy herself for all she was worth.

◆□◆□◆□◆□◆

"Gah!"

"Good-bye."

The last of the players turned to light.

Sally sheathed her daggers and sat down.

Several parties had come in, but none of them had even scratched her.

The sixth day was drawing to a close.

"Only thirty minutes left…"

It had been a while since the last attack. The time was eleven thirty PM.

Once Maple had her skills back, they could spend the seventh day doing whatever they wanted.

They could stay holed up in this dungeon or venture back into the wilds outside.

"Bet this is the last fight of the day!" Sally said, standing up and drawing her daggers.

She could hear footsteps approaching.

"Mm?"

"…Oh."

The intruder and Sally stood face-to-face.

It was a solo player.

In a kimono. With a katana.

"We meet again!"

"Sigh…what are *you* doing here, Kasumi?"

The newcomer turned out to be a familiar face.

Kasumi's hand went nowhere near her hilt.

Clearly not looking for a fight.

Sally was equally disinclined.

She would've fought back if Kasumi attacked, but…they *had* cleared a dungeon together.

It wasn't like Sally was interested in starting anything.

"I've got a gold medal already," Kasumi explained. "I figured it was time I started hiding."

"That's why we're here!"

"So Maple's farther in? I wondered."

"She's holed up at the back."

"Mind if I say hello?"

"Unless you can wade through poison, you'll die instantly."

This told Kasumi everything she needed to know. She elected not to proceed further.

"She'll come out soon enough," Sally said. "She's holding all our medals, so…I'm in here clearing any players who come in searching for some."

Kasumi nodded. "Mind if I join you?" she asked. "I was getting targeted a lot out there…"

Most players knew Kasumi by sight, so her encounters had largely led to immediate combat.

"Sure. Anyone comes your way, cut 'em down!"

"Certainly. I don't wish to lose my gold medal, either."

Now there were *two* mid-bosses.

With Kasumi here, far less players would mistake them for monsters.

But it added the lure of a gold medal…so the odds of them fighting remained just as high.

They chatted awhile, one eye on the passage leading in—and then Maple emerged from behind.

"Sally! They leveled up! Looky, looky! Syrup got a new skill… Oh?"

She came running out of the back, Syrup and Oboro on her heels.

And then her eyes met Kasumi's.

"Kasumi?! Why are *you* here?!"

"Uh…well, just trying to protect my medal… What are those?"

Kasumi was the first player to see either of their pets.

"Our new partners!"

They hadn't actually told Kasumi the bird boss story last time, so they filled her in.

"Eggs as a reward? I assume you're the only two who have those. I've met a lot of players and have never seen anything like them."

Kasumi was right.

Only Maple and Sally had pet monsters.

Perhaps there would be more after future events, but it would almost certainly require clearing extremely difficult dungeons.

"Oh, right, here's Oboro back."

"Mm, thanks."

They put their rings back the way they were.

"Well? Ready to ditch this cave?"

It was already after midnight.

Maple was back in action, so they didn't need to hole up to survive anymore.

But Maple wasn't really feeling the need.

She was more inclined to be cautious and protect their medals.

And she told Sally as much.

"Then...go on and block that passage for us."

"Sure thing!"

Maple moved to the door and drew New Moon.

It felt like ages since she'd seen that big ole purple circle.

"Hydra!"

The poison dragon raced off toward the entrance, splattering the walls and floor in its wake.

It also swallowed an approaching party and tore the face off a player peering in the entrance—but Maple never noticed.

She just walked halfway down the passage, deployed Venom Capsule, and then came back.

"Now we're totally safe!"

"And Kasumi and I are trapped in here!"

"Oh, good point. Well...I trust you both."

Kasumi had no escape.

So they *could* steal her medal.

The girls glanced at each other. Maple shook her head. The meaning of that wasn't lost on Sally. They were dead set on not fighting.

"Just one more day to burn!"

Probably best to get some sleep.

No need to spend the last day exhausted.

Just in case, they still slept in shifts, one of them keeping watch while the other two crashed.

But morning came without any intruders.

Every now and then, someone with Poison Resist did risk a step into the cave entrance—and promptly died.

"Mornin'."

"Morning!"

"Good morning. Just one more day."

The long event was drawing to a close.

Maple and Sally had achieved their goal and were thoroughly satisfied.

"Oh, right! You never know when we might need these medals. Sally, you want yours?"

Maple took Sally's share from her inventory and handed them over.

"Thanks."

Sally accepted them and stowed them safely away.

Kasumi had been more invested in protecting her gold medal than finding silver ones, so she didn't have nearly as many.

"But spending the whole day here could get a little boring."

"True."

"Maple, you brought a bunch of games, right? Those could help."

Maple nodded and took them all out.

Including Othello.

"Kanade was *so* good…," she said, remembering her losses.

They'd promised to play again sometime.

"Kanade?" Kasumi asked.

Maple told her the story. That segued naturally to the giant squid fight, which astonished Kasumi all the more.

Not many players had gone up against as many fearsome foes as these two.

"Are you sure you aren't just *bad* at Othello?" Sally asked. "Wanna play me?"

"Hnggg… Okay, I've gotta prove myself now!"

"You're on!"

Maple picked black and Sally, white.

The results…

…nearly every piece wound up black.

"Uh…Maple, how are you so good?"

"See? I know my 'thello. Kanade's just better!"

"Yeah, yeah. Let's go with something all three of us can play next."

Sally wasn't about to take this loss lying down but had zero problems switching to a different game.

It was clear she stood no chance at Othello.

No other players interrupted their games.

And in time…

The event approached its end.

The announcement echoed across the entire map. A five-minute warning that they were about to be transported back to the main game.

That meant no more Kasumi.

"See you post-event."

"Yeah, we should meet up again."

New friends and new powers.

As the curtains fell, both girls deemed the event a complete success.

CHAPTER 12

Defense Build and Skill Selection

When the event concluded, they were sent back to the square they'd started in.

And the flow of time returned to normal.

The announcement from the admins said the exchange of medals for skills would happen in thirty minutes, so if any medal redistribution had to happen, they should handle it now.

Maple had already given Sally her share, so they were taken care of.

"I wonder what skills they'll have?"

"We'll just have to find out."

Half an hour later…

There was another announcement, informing participants they'd be transported to private rooms for the selection process. There would be no discussing things with other party members, so each player would have to pick skills that seemed right for them.

Anyone with more than ten medals was wreathed in light and vanished.

Anyone with less would simply carry those medals over to the next event.

*　　*　　*

Maple's view was blocked by a screen—the same blue as her stat window.

She found herself in a room with no doors—nothing but the screen.

She stepped closer to it and saw a list of skill names.

Tapping a skill brought up a description box.

"Um… There's, like, a hundred of them…"

Combat skills, crafting skills, stat boosts, and skills that didn't fit any of those categories.

Row after row.

"Doesn't seem like I have a time limit…so I guess I'll be thorough!"

Maple had enough medals for two skills. She didn't have any need for combat skills, so she skipped past those.

Lots of skills had names like Holy Sword Arts or Dragon Spear, meaning they were obviously not for her.

And her Dexterity was too low for any crafting skills.

That narrowed down the list of skills she could actually take.

In fact, of all the players with medals, Maple had the least skill options that would actually be relevant to her build.

But that meant less time mulling it over.

"Resist All… But Fortress is also good. Or maybe just plain Magic Boost…"

Maple had a short list, but…

"Mm? Hmm…"

One other skill caught her attention.

She stared at the description so hard, it was like she was trying to bore a hole into it with her eyes.

"O-okay! Definitely taking that one," she decided.

She'd felt a flash of inspiration, and she let that sweep her along.

"Now, what about the other one?"

She looked through the full list again. If she found something else inspiring, she decided she'd go for it.

"Anything else...um..."

But nothing else really leaped out at her. After some thought, she picked Fortress.

Fortress was a simple skill, giving her one and a half times VIT.

Activating it carried no disadvantages—it seemed well worth the medals.

Maple already had similar skills, but that was because Maple's build was far from ordinary.

Either way, once she'd made her selection, she was enveloped in light and disappeared.

The day after the event...

The usual crowd gathered on the forums.

---

542 Name: Anonymous Great Shielder
Event's done!
So much to talk about.

543 Name: Anonymous Greatsworder
Done and dusted!
Superlong.

544 Name: Anonymous Spear Master
Only two hours real time!
Kinda a weird feeling.

545 Name: Anonymous Great Shielder
I know!

546 Name: Anonymous Greatsworder
Anyone nab ten medals?
I sure couldn't.

547 Name: Anonymous Mage
Nope.
Those dungeons were rough!
And seven days of exploration takes its toll.

548 Name: Anonymous Spear Master
Truth.

549 Name: Anonymous Greatsworder
We climbed the tallest peak, but there was nothing up there. So
exhausting...

550 Name: Anonymous Great Shielder
The tall one with a circular clearing on top?
There was a shrine, though, right?

551 Name: Anonymous Greatsworder
Oh, yeah. That's the one.
You know anything?

552 Name: Anonymous Spear Master
I'm curious.

553 Name: Anonymous Mage

Tell us more!

554 Name: Anonymous Great Shielder
OK.
Long story, but here goes.
We climbed it, too.
There was a magic circle by the shrine.

We stepped on it, and inside was a bird monster that roflstomped us.
Like, complete devastation.

It generated so much hail, we couldn't see through it. Totally melted us.
Completely ludicrous DPS.

But if you got to the top and found nothing, someone must have
taken it down.

555 Name: Anonymous Greatsworder
Huh?
No way.
Unless it had like, 1 HP...

556 Name: Anonymous Spear Master
I mean, you're Chrome, right?
If you can't do it, then who...?
Oh, wait. I see where this is going.

557 Name: Anonymous Mage
I know this one girl...

558 Name: Anonymous Great Shielder

I ain't done yet!
There was this other party on the peak with us...

And it was Maple and a friend, I think? They were together.

She was in all-blue gear, cool and cute.

So if the magic circle vanished...
Odds are those two cleared it.
They must've gone in after us.

559 Name: Anonymous Greatsworder
Yeah, those two could maybe pull it off.
Maple just tanks her way through.
Or maybe this friend (?) of hers is a big monster.
What do we think?

560 Name: Anonymous Archer
Sorry I'm late
But I do have two valuable bits of intel.

561 Name: Anonymous Great Shielder
Like what?

562 Name: Anonymous Mage
C'mon!
Nothing's gonna shock me now.

563 Name: Anonymous Archer
First
The event's sixth day had a mass slaughter

Like a humanoid monster in blue roaming around...
May have been a player?

Either way, nobody saw her use a skill, but she dodged every attack,
came right in for the kill.
Folks claim she vanished into thin air or their blades twisted to
avoid her...
And she took down a *lot* of people.

And then later on, the same girl was acting like a mid-boss in a cave
nearby.
And I saw a post claim that a Hydra came out of that same cave.

564 Name: Anonymous Great Shielder
I get ya
Blue gear, huh?
And a Hydra.
Sounds familiar.

565 Name: Anonymous Greatsworder
That Hydra is def Maple
Can't be two of her!
So then, uh...
Blue Gear's her friend?

566 Name: Anonymous Mage
Sounds likely.
Which means she's also broken.
Humans can't just dodge swords mid-swing.

567 Name: Anonymous Spear Master

And it was during the event, so not even a medal skill.

Maybe one with unknown acquisition conditions?

Or...just her own raw gaming ability.

Which makes her superhuman.

568 Name: Anonymous Great Shielder

Oh, speaking of medal skills

One of those seemed like it might be the root cause of Maple's super defense.

Fortress.

Gives VIT x 1.5

Odds are she's stacking several skills like that.

One wouldn't be enough.

1.5 my VIT wouldn't do it—that's for sure.

569 Name: Anonymous Mage

Maybe Maple took that

No, she definitely did.

We know she had at least one gold medal.

So she's become even tankier?!

570 Name: Anonymous Archer

Back to my intel, part two!

After the event, I spotted Maple and her friend in the desert.

I was all, oh, Maple, been a while...

But she was riding around on a flying turtle, making it rain poison.

571 Name: Anonymous Mage
Stop, can't process

572 Name: Anonymous Great Shielder
There's no skill like that
There can't be
Is there?
I don't even know anymore

573 Name: Anonymous Greatsworder
Seriously, how many medals did she get?
How would that even be possible?

574 Name: Anonymous Archer
I have no clue
Weirdness:
Turtle
Flying
Poison rain
Triple crazy

Even if we chalk up poison rain as "typical Maple," that still leaves
two insane things!
What happened during this event?!

575 Name: Anonymous Spear Master
There's no taming skill
Wait
Unless that was an event item?

576 Name: Anonymous Great Shielder

Maple's earning herself nicknames left and right.
People already called her a Fortress...
But we gotta change that.
She's a Flying Fortress now.

577 Name: Anonymous Mage
Take your eyes off her for a second and she goes flying away
I'd kill to see her skill and equip lists.
She's literally a Flying Fortress now.
I assume there's gotta be time limits?

578 Name: Anonymous Greatsworder
Keep an eye on her friend, too.
Anyone grouping up with Maple's gotta be a bit bonkers.

579 Name: Anonymous Archer
I'm sure she ain't run-of-the-mill anything, yeah.
I'd like to fight her myself.
Maybe there's some gnarly skill out there that makes attacks miss.
Can't tell how bad it is without fighting her myself.

580 Name: Anonymous Great Shielder
I'll approach 'em soonish, then.
I'm on Maple's friend list, after all.
See if I can scope out this friend of hers while I'm at it.

581 Name: Anonymous Spear Master
Waiting for your report, then.

582 Name: Anonymous Greatsworder
Looking forward to it!

◆□◆□◆◆□◆□◆

"What skill did you choose, Sally?"

They were sitting on a bench in the second stratum's town, having picked their medal skills.

"Hmm, I thought about it for a while, then took Chaser Blade."

"Chaser Blade?"

Maple hadn't even read the attack skill descriptions, so she didn't know what it did.

"Uh, so if you attack with a weapon successfully, it adds an extra attack at one third strength."

"Um…"

"It basically doubles the hits I do. Since I dual wield, that means Double Slash now does eight hits."

"Wow!"

"Of course, I also have Jack of All Trades, and dual wielding lowers the damage from both hits, so it'll be a while before that really starts to matter."

Sally favored swift hits and lots of them.

Maple favored raising her durability.

"What'd you grab, Maple?"

"I also got a skill that might not be useful!"

"Huh?"

This confused Sally.

Why would she take a skill if she wasn't sure it would work?

"Can we hit up the desert? I wanna try this where no one'll see."

"Uh, sure…okay…"

Sally couldn't begin to imagine what skill Maple had picked.

"All righty, come on out, Syrup!"

Maple summoned her pet.

"Syrup! Giganticize!"

At her order, Syrup's body was wreathed in light—and enlarged.

It was now three yards tall.

And five and a half yards long.

This was a skill Syrup had learned on the sixth day, after leveling up.

Giganticize

Doubles HP.

The giant version had twice the health but was also a bigger target—so it would take more overall damage. Without much in the way of speed, this was not a great skill for Syrup to have right now.

"Please work…please work…"

Maple had her eyes closed and her hands clasped together in prayer.

She remained like that for a minute; then her eyes opened, gleaming.

"Psychokinesis!"

At her cry…Syrup's body *levitated*.

Ignoring all the weight its bulk would imply, Syrup wafted upward, hovering a good ten yards overhead.

"Wha—?"

"Yes! Yes! It worked!"

Maple was jumping for joy.

Meanwhile, Sally's jaw had dropped. The girl who'd kept her cool all through the giant bird fight was completely floored.

She could see for herself what had happened, but it had banished all rational thought from her mind.

Maple had picked this skill on a hunch and nothing more.
Sally could never do that.
But that was how you discovered the truly absurd.

The skill Maple had chosen was not, at a glance, something
Maple would ever want.

Psychokinesis

Makes monsters levitate.
Skill success varies depending on the monster's
resistance.
If it fails, that monster cannot be targeted again for one
hour.
Can be used only on monsters.
MP required varies based on target's resistance level.

Even when Maple showed her the skill, Sally was still baffled.
The skill description contained nothing that would explain
why Maple had picked it.
To Sally's eyes, it read like a skill that would immobilize an
enemy, but even then, it had only a *chance* of doing so, at a poten-
tially steep cost.
"Why did you take this?" she asked.
"I thought it might let me fly around on Syrup!"
"Ohhh, right."
There *was no* deeper reason.
Maple had just thought it sounded *fun*. She wanted to fly, so she
had chosen a skill that might let her.

And, as previously demonstrated, Maple's gut instincts could sometimes create the most fiendish results.

"Uh, Maple...how long can Syrup fly?"

"Er...wow, good question."

Maple checked her MP. It wasn't draining at all.

"..............You're kidding me."

"What? You figure something out?"

"Syrup isn't your typical monster. It's bound to you via the Bonding Bridge."

"Yup! And?"

Maple was, of course, wearing that ring.

"So with that ring...and with you two being connected...would it have *any* resistance?"

Sally figured the Bonding Bridge would cancel that out.

And if the resist rate was 0 percent, how much MP would that take?

The skill description hadn't specified, so Sally had overlooked it.

She wasn't the type to waste good medals on a long shot.

"So...this means I can fly around on Syrup a lot?"

"Uh...yeah."

"Then to heck with the details! Syrup! Come back down!"

Maple's pet returned to her.

"Put me on your back!"

Syrup's jaws closed around Maple's head, and it tossed her in the air.

"Oof!"

She landed on its shell with a *clang*. The shell was large enough to be pretty comfortable.

Maple had Syrup rise up a bit, maybe seven yards off the ground. She looked around.

"Maple! Pill bugs incoming!"

Maple heard Sally yelling from down below.

She looked around and saw the sand plumes rising as the pill bugs rolled in.

"Stay back, Sally!" she called.

Instantly realizing Maple was about to try something, Sally used Superspeed to get out of Dodge.

There was no telling *what* was about to go down.

"Acid Rain!"

Maple aimed New Moon at the sky.

A magic circle appeared, spawning six-inch-wide balls of purple water that fell randomly in a ten-yard radius around Maple.

"Rain away! Rain today!" Maple sang. Each time her toxic shower struck a pill bug, it stopped moving.

And if they weren't darting around, their destruction was inevitable.

There were two figures watching this from a distance.

One was Sally.

The other was a man with a bow.

""Wow...""

Maple's arcane exploits were enough to demolish anyone's vocabulary.

Defense Build and Admins 4

Not long after...

The number of players selecting skills hit zero, and everyone leaned back in their chairs.

This was the admin room.

Everyone looked exhausted.

Ready to fall asleep in their chairs.

"Okay! Everyone's picked their skills."

"Whew...this event was grueling. Thank god there were no bugs."

"Unless we count Maple. At least she solved the puzzle before taking down the Sea Emperor. That was a huge relief..."

"I was getting really scared she'd take out the full-strength version."

"If she had, she would've made off with the bird and the wolf, too..."

"Yeah...no telling how she might've bulldozed her way through it."

"Mm. Let's chalk that up as a win."

"*Sigh...* Oh, right! What skills did Maple pick?"

"I'm sure she went for Fortress, at least. Right? Please tell me she did."

"Yeah, she grabbed Fortress. No problems there. Her defense is already so bonkers, further increases won't make a... Wait... Psycho...kinesis?"

"Why does that sound so ominous?"

"I'm quaking."

"Locate Maple! Put her on-screen now!"

Maple appeared on the screen.

And they all saw...

...Maple riding a giant flying turtle, making it rain poison.

""...Crap.""

"I said to double-check every skill! You all heard me!"

"I—I did check them!" another admin wailed. "It just never occurred to me that Maple would pick *that*! I figured it didn't need any tinkering..."

""You got complacent!""

"Anything is possible with Maple! This is just her being normal!"

"Arghhhhhhhh! Auuughhhhhhhhhhh!"

The images on-screen were so shocking, several weary admins passed out on the spot.

Eventually resignation set in, and they turned off the screen. Everyone was too tired to do anything else.

Defense Build and the Spoils of Battle

"Ha! I got 'em all!"

Maple made Syrup descend.

She tried to carefully climb down but wound up taking a tumble.

She returned Syrup to her ring and went over to Sally.

"I'm back!"

"You have evolved beyond my wildest imaginings, Maple."

"I have?"

"Yup."

During the second event, they'd obtained a great shield and some scrolls.

Both from the cave of snails.

They'd put them away, planning to check them out later, and had totally forgotten about them until now.

Would these help Maple evolve even further?

"Let's see the scrolls first."

These scrolls allowed them to learn a skill called Inspire.

Kasumi had one, too.

Inspire

Increases STR and AGI by 20% for one minute for all party members within a 15-yard range.
Does not affect user.

"A party skill… I can't see myself getting much use out of it," Sally said.

Raising these stats wouldn't benefit Maple at all.

Any percentage buff to 0 was still 0.

If it buffed VIT, that might change, but these two stats were pointless.

But Sally figured it couldn't hurt to learn it anyway.

And it was definitely worth Maple's while.

"Next, the shield."

They'd given Kasumi the wand and spear for it. The shield was made of purple crystal.

It immediately summoned vivid memories of the snail-filled cavern.

"The walls all looked like this!"

"Yeah…if it weren't for those snails, I might even want to visit again someday."

Maple checked the great shield's stats.

Amethyst Geode

[VIT +30] [Crystal Wall]

She tapped the skill name.

The VIT boost was less than White Snow, so the skill would determine this shield's value.

Crystal Wall

Generates a wall around the user five yards in diameter.
The wall's HP matches the player's.
Five-minute cooldown after use.

"Hmm, might be useful, might not."

If it was based on VIT, it would be terrifying.

Every five minutes, Maple would have been able to summon a wall as tanky as herself.

"If your HP was higher, it would be pretty good."

Each stat point you put in HP raised it by 20. Same for MP.

Because of this, most players didn't go for Maple's pure defense build; instead, they raised their HP and did whatever it took to get themselves some HP recovery skills. This normally carried better chances for survival.

And the main reason why there weren't many defense builds.

You had to hit Maple's territory before VIT alone would break the damage system.

"I guess I'll try it out sometime," Maple said, putting the shield back in her inventory.

She figured the skill might come in handy someday.

"That's really the only shield you need, huh?" Sally said, pointing at Night's Facsimile.

They'd be hard-pressed to find another shield that good.

"Oh, and I leveled up."

"So did I! I killed all those fish while you were playing with the squid."

Maple

Lv29   HP 40/40 <+160>   MP 12/12 <+10>

[STR 0]   [VIT 180 <+141>]
[AGI 0]   [DEX 0]
[INT 0]

Equipment

Head	[None]	Body	[Black Rose Armor]
R. Hand	[New Moon: Hydra]	L. Hand	[Night's Facsimile: Devour]
Legs	[Black Rose Armor]	Feet	[Black Rose Armor]
Accessories	[Bonding Bridge]		
	[Toughness Ring]		
	[Life Ring]		

Skills

Shield Attack, Sidestep, Deflect, Meditation, Taunt, Inspire

HP Boost (S), MP Boost (S)

Great Shield Mastery IV, Cover Move I, Cover

Absolute Defense, Moral Turpitude, Giant Killing, Hydra Eater, Bomb Eater, Indomitable Guardian

Psychokinesis, Fortress

Sally

Lv24   HP 32/32   MP 45/45 <+35>

[STR 35 <+20>]   [VIT 0]
[AGI 85 <+68>]   [DEX 25 <+20>]
[INT 30 <+20>]

Equipment

Head	[Surface Scarf: Mirage]	Body	[Oceanic Coat: Oceanic]
R. Hand	[Deep Sea Dagger]	L. Hand	[Seabed Dagger]
Legs	[Oceanic Clothes]	Feet	[Black Boots]
Accessories	[Bonding Bridge]		
	[None]		
	[None]		

Skills

Slash, Double Slash, Gale Slash, Defense Break, Inspire
Down Attack, Power Attack, Switch Attack
Fire Ball, Water Ball, Wind Cutter, Cyclone Cutter
Sand Cutter, Dark Ball
Water Wall, Wind Wall, Refresh, Heal
Affliction III
Strength Boost (S), Combo Boost (S), Martial Arts V
MP Boost (S), MP Cost Down (S), MP Recovery Speed
Boost (S), Poison Resist (S)
Gathering Speed Boost (S)

Dagger Mastery II, Magic Mastery II
Fire Magic I, Water Magic II, Wind Magic III
Earth Magic I, Dark Magic I, Light Magic II
Combo Blade II, Presence Block II, Presence Detect II,
Sneaky Steps I, Leap III
Fishing, Swimming X, Diving X, Cooking I, Jack of All
Trades, Superspeed, Ancient Ocean, Chaser Blade

"I'm almost level thirty!"

"I'm trying real hard, but I'm not exactly closing the gap."

"What's the highest level anyone has?"

"Before the event, it was sixty-one, I think? The cap's at one hundred right now. But they'll probably raise it once the top player gets there."

"Sixty-one?! Wow...that's amazing. I don't think we're catching up to whoever that is anytime soon."

"People like that are in a league of their own. I mean...so are you, but..."

Sally herself was already earning a similar reputation.

Since there'd been no broadcast of this event, she wasn't *that* well-known yet, but simply being with Maple was enough to get attention, and in time, people would learn just how good she was.

"Back to school tomorrow... Feels like we're coming off a vacation."

"Yeah. Maybe we should log out early tonight?"

"Mm. Sounds good."

Both girls hit the log-out button...

And light filled their vision.

* * *

Back in the real world, Kaede checked the time.

"…It really was only two hours!"

It took a physical clock to make that feel convincing.

If she closed her eyes, everything that had happened during the weeklong event came flooding back to her.

So many tough fights. But she and Risa had had a lot of fun together.

"I wonder when the next event will be. Hopefully this time, Kasumi and Kanade can join in."

Kaede savored the memories a moment longer but then moved over to the desk to get ready for tomorrow.

"Did Risa do her homework? I bet she went right to sleep."

She figured she'd better text Risa a reminder—didn't want her to get banned from games again—but then a thought struck her.

"Wow…I really am addicted now."

Kaede had caught herself wanting to spend more time gaming with Risa—and a similar impulse was what had led Risa to invite her to this game in the first place.

And she'd wound up thoroughly corrupted.

"Now I get why she was so dead set on convincing me to join her!"

She'd have to say as much tomorrow. But for now, she had to focus on her homework.

AFTERWORD

If you started with the first volume, thanks for waiting! If you're just joining us, welcome aboard! I'm Yuumikan.

Your support has made a second volume of *I Don't Want to Get Hurt, so I'll Max Out My Defense* possible.

It's thanks to you that we were able to get a second volume out so fast.

I was very relieved when they had to do a second printing of the first volume right after release.

Having a book physically in your hands really drives home how much you've actually written.

But…seeing them all lined up in the store is a very strange feeling.

It's like it's no longer yours.

Something that once seemed like a distant realm is suddenly close to home.

Maybe I'll get used to that feeling in time…if people keep supporting the series and I get to keep putting out more volumes.

But right now, I feel like I'll never get used to it.

*   *   *

In fact, I think it's good to stay a little nervous. I'll never be the type to act like I own the place.

But yeah. The first volume brought me all kinds of new emotions.

And working on *Bofuri*, Vol. 2 brought a lot of new experiences, as novel as they were challenging.

Trimming things down is even harder than adding new material. And I'm sure I caused a lot of headaches in the process.

All of this is still very new to me, and all the more fulfilling as a result.

Looking back, I first posted the material in *Bofuri*, Vol. 2 over a year ago. Readers who have been with me from the start may even find they've forgotten half of it.

KOIN drew some fabulous illustrations, and my editor helped improve the pacing.

I hope those readers will enjoy this new version and the differences it brings.

And like I did in Volume 1, I'd better bring the second volume of *I Don't Want to Get Hurt, so I'll Max Out My Defense* to a close.

If good fortune came my way once...

...and even twice, then the third time's got to be the charm.

Let's hope that saying's true!

And look forward to meeting again in Volume 3.

Yuumikan

HAVE YOU BEEN TURNED ON TO LIGHT NOVELS YET?

IN STORES NOW!

SWORD ART ONLINE, VOL. 1-22
SWORD ART ONLINE PROGRESSIVE 1-6

The chart-topping light novel series that spawned the explosively popular anime and manga adaptations!

MANGA ADAPTATION AVAILABLE NOW!

SWORD ART ONLINE © Reki Kawahara ILLUSTRATION: abec
KADOKAWA CORPORATION ASCII MEDIA WORKS

ACCEL WORLD, VOL. 1-24

Prepare to accelerate with an action-packed cyber-thriller from the bestselling author of *Sword Art Online*.

MANGA ADAPTATION AVAILABLE NOW!

ACCEL WORLD © Reki Kawahara ILLUSTRATION: HIMA
KADOKAWA CORPORATION ASCII MEDIA WORKS

SPICE AND WOLF, VOL. 1-21

A disgruntled goddess joins a traveling merchant in this light novel series that inspired the *New York Times* bestselling manga.

MANGA ADAPTATION AVAILABLE NOW!

SPICE AND WOLF © Isuna Hasekura ILLUSTRATION: Jyuu Ayakura
KADOKAWA CORPORATION ASCII MEDIA WORKS

IS IT WRONG TO TRY TO PICK UP GIRLS IN A DUNGEON?, VOL. 1-15

A would-be hero turns damsel in distress in this hilarious send-up of sword-and-sorcery tropes.

MANGA ADAPTATION AVAILABLE NOW!

Is It Wrong to Try to Pick Up Girls in a Dungeon? © Fujino Omori / SB Creative Corp.

IS IT WRONG TO TRY TO PICK UP GIRLS IN A DUNGEON? 1

FUJINO OMORI
ILLUSTRATION BY SUZUHITO YASUDA

ANOTHER

The spine-chilling horror novel that took Japan by storm is now available in print for the first time in English—in a gorgeous hardcover edition.

MANGA ADAPTATION AVAILABLE NOW!

Another © Yukito Ayatsuji 2009/ KADOKAWA CORPORATION, Tokyo

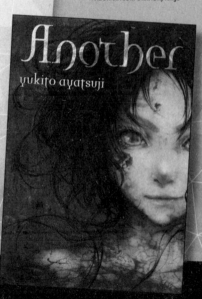

Another
yukito ayatsuji

A CERTAIN MAGICAL INDEX, VOL. 1-22

Science and magic collide as Japan's most popular light novel franchise makes its English-language debut.

MANGA ADAPTATION AVAILABLE NOW!

A CERTAIN MAGICAL INDEX © Kazuma Kamachi
ILLUSTRATION: Kiyotaka Haimura
KADOKAWA CORPORATION ASCII MEDIA WORKS

1
KAZUMA KAMACHI
ILLUSTRATED BY
KIYOTAKA HAIMURA

A Certain Magical Index

VISIT YENPRESS.COM TO CHECK OUT ALL THE TITLES IN OUR NEW LIGHT NOVEL INITIATIVE AND...

GET YOUR YEN ON!

www.YenPress.com

BOFURI : i don't WANT to GET HURT, so i'll MAX OUT my DEFENSE.

**YOU'VE READ THE LIGHT NOVEL,
NOW STREAM THE ANIME ON FUNIMATION!**

funimation.com/bofuri

**ALSO OWN THE
SEASON 1 LIMITED EDITION
ON BLU-RAY, DVD & DIGITAL**

Funimation ©2020 Yuumikan-Koin/KADOKAWA/Bofuri Project. Licensed by Funimation® Global Group, LLC. All Rights Reserved.